"EXQUISITELY CRAFTED, DREAMLIKE . . .
Oates powerfully creates a hallucinatory and harrowing
atmosphere charged with sensuality and destruction."
—*Publishers Weekly*

"Calla is Sister Carrie (a contemporary, not
coincidentally) forced by temperament to do battle
with forces impossibly oversized and hopelessly
immovable. And yet none of these circumstances can
minimize Ms. Oates' creation, or her accomplishment
in this short novel. She has contemplated an artist's
faded image and brought it fully to life."
—*The New York Times Book Review*

"For whatever else this little book may be—fiction on
art, or an artfully composed shadowbox of narrative
within narrative—it is first a singular and affecting
story: an American village tale of passion suppressed
by obdurate convention past the point of endurance,
even past the point where language avails. . . . A stirring
book."   —Richard Ford

"Oates provides Khnopff's haunting work of art,
featured on the cover, with an eloquent voice in this
breathless, shadowy tale."   —*Kirkus Reviews*

JOYCE CAROL OATES is the author of twenty-one novels,
as well as short stories, poems, essays, and plays, most recently *Because It Is Bitter, and Because It Is My Heart*
(Plume) and *Heat* (Dutton). She is a member of The American Academy and Institute of Arts and Letters, and has been
honored by a National Book Award for Fiction, among
many other awards. She is currently the Roger S. Berlind
Distinguished Professor in the Humanities at Princeton Uni-
versity.

I
LOCK
MY
DOOR
UPON
MYSELF

Joyce Carol Oates

A PLUME BOOK

PLUME
Published by the Penguin Group
Penguin Books USA Inc., 375 Hudson Street, New York, New York 10014, U.S.A.
Penguin Books Ltd, 27 Wrights Lane, London W8 5TZ, England
Penguin Books Australia Ltd, Ringwood, Victoria, Australia
Penguin Books Canada Ltd, 10 Alcorn Avenue,
Toronto, Ontario, Canada M4V 3B2
Penguin Books (N.Z.) Ltd, 182-190 Wairau Road, Auckland 10, New Zealand

Penguin Books Ltd, Registered Offices: Harmondsworth, Middlesex, England

Published by Plume, an imprint of New American Library, a division of Penguin Books
USA Inc. This is an authorized reprint of a hardcover edition published by The Ecco Press.

First Plume Printing, December, 1991
10 9 8 7 6 5 4 3 2 1

 REGISTERED TRADEMARK—MARCA REGISTRADA

LIBRARY OF CONGRESS CATALOGING-IN-PUBLICATION DATA
Oates, Joyce Carol, 1938–
    I lock my door upon myself / Joyce Carol Oates.
        p.   cm.
    ISBN 0-452-26708-0
    I. Title.
    [PS3565.A8I18   1991]
    813′.54—dc20   91–26894
                                                        CIP

Printed in the United States of America
Original hardcover design by Nicola Mazzella

PUBLISHER'S NOTE
This is a work of fiction. Names, characters, places, and incidents either are the product
of the author's imagination or are used fictitiously, and any resemblance to actual persons,
living or dead, events, or locales is entirely coincidental.

again, for my parents Carolina and Frederic Oates,
and in memory of that world, now vanishing, that
continues to nourish . . .

I
LOCK
MY
DOOR
UPON
MYSELF

PART
I

1

. . . there on the river, the Chautauqua, in a sepia sun, the rowboat bucking the choppy waves with a look almost of gaiety, defiance. And in the boat the couple: the man, rowing, a black man, the woman a white woman whose face is too distant to be seen. The man is rowing the boat downstream in a slightly jagged course yet with energy, purpose, the oars like blades rising and dropping and rising and again dropping, sinking into the water only to emerge again dripping and impatient; the woman is facing him, close, their knees touching, or so it appears from shore . . . the woman sits straight, ramrod straight, in a posture of extreme attentiveness to the man's and the boat's every move. With one hand she clutches the lurching side of the boat to steady herself, the other hand is shut into a fist, white-knuckled, immobile, in her lap.

. . . past Milburn, past Flemingville, past Shaheen, and then they begin to be seen, to be remarked upon . . . but only when they are a mile above Tintern Falls do people begin to shout in warning and now even the cries of birds at the river's edge lift sharp and piercing with warning. Then about a half-mile above Tintern the rowboat is taken by the swift-flowing current as by a giant hand and now it would require the black man's most strenuous and desperate exertions to steer it from its course yet he lifts the oars and rests them calmly in place as the woman sits continuing to watch him closely, possibly smiling, are the two of them smiling?—talking together?—hearing nothing of the shouts from shore and nothing of the increasing roar of the falls ahead, the sixty-foot drop on the other side of the bridge and the churning white water beyond. . . .

2

That was 1912. Upstate New York in the Chautauqua River Valley, where dusk and then night come quickly because the steep surrounding cliffs and the foothills beyond cast such long still shadows across the land, it's as if the darkness, then the night, lift, then thicken, already there, even in the light, and waiting to take hold.

3

She was my mother's mother but not my grandmother in any terms I can comprehend and if her
mad blood courses through me now I have no knowledge
of it and am innocent of it.

"Calla": given that name by her own mother as soon
as she was born, in January 1890; as if her mother had
known in the agony of childbirth she could not live, thus
wanted to give her infant daughter, her first- and last-
born, a legacy suggestive of the grave.

So that even as a child my mother's mother was forced
to consider her name specially ordained, fated: a white
beyond white: the sweet waxy glaze of calla lilies, massed
funeral flowers.

4

Not "Calla" but "Edith Margaret" was my
mother's mother's baptismal name; the name that
appeared on official records and would one day appear, in
chiseled script, on her grave marker—in the Freilicht family plot of the First Lutheran Church of Shaheen, Eden
County, New York.

"Calla" was the name she insisted upon, as a child.
Speaking of herself in the third person, as if stating a fact

— "Calla wants to go outside, now," "Calla doesn't want to go to bed, she isn't sleepy" — though no one knew who'd told her about that name, given to her by her mother on her mother's deathbed.

From the first, Calla was a difficult child.

5

She had to be disciplined, sometimes hourly, she was that kind of child, too much energy, restlessness, had to be slapped, spanked, paddled. By her father, by her grandmother, by others. There were blows with open hands and blows with closed fists and also pummelings, hair pulling, even shouts of fury and frustration, screams. In those years there was no "abuse" of children, only "discipline."

There was never cruelty in the transaction, only justice.

So she learned to hold herself taut, rigid, her jaws locked against pleading or weeping, her eyes half shut so that milky crescents showed, inside which, stubborn too, vision itself seemed to withdraw; and squatting in front of her, gripping her shoulders, adults were infuriated by the child's refusal to acknowledge them.

My self is all to me. I don't have any need of you.

Once having been drinking hard mash cider for most of a day Calla's father passed a burning match close beneath his daughter's eyes but saw only the reflection of the flame in those eyes, closed to him.

He thought, "—She isn't mine."

For there was, too, the mere physical fact of her, the anomaly: on neither side of the family was there evidence of such flamey-red hair, thick as a horse's mane; such fine, nervous, aquiline features. Though each summer her skin burnt and eventually tanned her natural color was pale, bloodless, lightly freckled, with a look of translucence; her deeply set eyes were dark brown, so dark as to appear black in certain lights, without any distinction between iris and pupil.

The family said of her, "—If this one isn't ours, whose is she?"

6

In that remote farmhouse north of Milburn—by degrees ramshackle, derelict, and the life of the daily household disorganized—Calla grew up long-limbed, willful, unpredictable; cunning as a half-domesticated creature; so precocious in her manner she might have been, at age eight or nine, mistaken for a child of twelve. Her father was often absent (Albert Honeystone: a farmer forced by crop failures and the manipulation of grain markets wholly beyond his control or even his comprehension to sell off his forty acres of rich dark fertile

Chautauqua Valley soil in multi-acre parcels until only three acres remained and then he was a foreman at a saw-mill upriver and then a day laborer for the county, and a drinker of hard mash cider and homemade whiskey throughout), and the Honeystone grandparents were slowed by ailments, dazed and embittered country people with their only conviction a sense of the world veering off at angles inhospitable to their interests *No matter how hard you work, God damn bone-aching hard you work* so in that household Calla flourished like the hardiest and most practical of weeds, burdock, sunflower, taking root in any soil and once rooted impossible to extirpate, such households nourish us in ways we can't know and certainly no outsider could guess. Often she stayed out from school to tramp about the fields and woods and along the creek, gone sometimes for entire days when she'd show up at a neighbor's farm like a stray cat or dog *Oh is it Edith Honeystone?* and she'd say *I'm Calla* in that low assured matter-of-fact voice, not so much certain of herself and of her welcome as indifferent; simply not caring; as ready to turn and wander back into the woods as to come into a house and be fed like any normal child.

She grew up devouring, not meals, but food: if at home rarely sitting down at the table and as often outdoors as in.

Eating in the barn with the animals *Oh she's an animal herself—that one.*

She was quickly bored, thus feverish, mutinous, in the single-room country schoolhouse fashioned of crudely hewn logs children from the district were obliged to attend from first through eighth grade, or until the age of sixteen: these wildly disparate grades taught by a female instructor of ravaged middle age who nonetheless had the strength not only to hold such precociously strong children as Calla Honeystone in place as they struggled but to discipline them with swift smarting blows from a willow branch; all but a few times able to prevent them from wresting the branch out of her fingers and striking her with it.

As Calla did, once, with such alacrity and aplomb the other students, even the six-foot-tall farm boys at the rear of the classroom, were astonished: wresting the whipping branch out of Mrs. Vogel's fingers and striking her with it full in the face so that her round wire-rimmed glasses went flying *So you can see how she had to be disciplined, just an animal a wild animal just white trash from above Milburn.*

7

The father went off. Joined up with the Army, or drifted west. Or got sick and died in some city where no one knew him or cared so he was buried in a pauper's grave and no one back in Milburn knew, and about this time, in Calla's thirteenth year, she became religious suddenly, though she had long resisted being forced to attend services at the little Methodist church nine miles away in the village of Shaheen where the minister, Reverend Bogey, sometimes wept recalling the sufferings

of Christ and the wickedness of the Devil masquerading as
mortal men in our midst *Oh he is everywhere—he is legion,*
and one week Calla Honeystone sat smirking and chewing
her lip and the next there she was crying too, an angry
kind of crying, and the tears hot looking and the pale
freckled face hot too. Everyone was astonished at the girl's
ferocity, how passionately she sang the hymns in her wavering contralto voice, how she began to excel in Sunday
school memorizing Bible verses recited with the conviction of kindling sticks burning and crackling and
she began to speak of God and of Jesus Christ as if they
were in the room with her, bodiless and invisible yet
somehow present, active presences. There was a quarrel-
some edge to it. People spoke of Calla's face as "radiant,"
"unearthly." She learned to play the pump organ, just the
rudiments required for playing chords, accompanying the
congregation as they sang and she sang too, *for if there is
God and if there is Jesus Christ aren't they always with us?—
inside us and outside us?—maybe all of us are dead and this is the
resurrection?*

8

So maybe, years later, when my mother's mother
began her retreat—"retreat" is a way of looking at
it, "exile" might be another—remaining within a single
house for a period of fifty-five years *Yes it is unimaginable:*

that is why I must imagine it there was this precedent of a kind; this consolation that is beyond mere religious belief, or the wish to believe; a conviction, whether mystical, or simply mad, that God is all in all and inside us and outside us in equal measure, thus why would it matter where one was, in any literal geographical sense?—why, even, who one was?

Who one *is.* Since of course, in God, you don't die.

9

But God did not summon Albert Honeystone back nor did He prevent what little remained of the farm from being taken over entirely by the Yewville Bank & Trust and in pitiless slipping-down degrees He oversaw the tumor-death of first the grandfather and then the grandmother and there was Calla Honeystone tall and skinny yet thriving, her fierce eyes and her amazing hair the color of orange poppies and her prolonged silence—for days, maybe for a week, so they worried she might be mentally defective and then what would they do?—when she went to live with relatives of her dead mother's in the village of Shaheen: this girl so mature in their eyes she might as easily have passed for twenty years of age as for fourteen; who might have been of unusual intelligence and sensitivity as plausibly as she might have been touched in the head.

"Touched in the head": Calla knew what people whispered behind her back, even her mother's people, and she was both outraged in her pride and strangely pleased for, somehow, yes she liked that thought, that idea, "touched" by the finger of God Himself: compelled to live out a special destiny none of the fools and idiots and commonplace sinners around her could guess.

10

At that time—this was 1905, 1906—it was common practice for banks foreclosing mortgages on certain farm properties to board up the house and outbuildings until the auction was held, sometimes even to raze the house so that the evicted family in their desperation would not creep back by stealth to take up a vagabond residence in their former home; sleeping as criminals on floorboards they themselves had laid, furtively gathering weed-stunted produce they themselves had planted, pumping water from their own wells now forbidden to them under pain of arrest for trespassing.

If they'd done that to me or even tried I would have killed them. Killed whoever. Whoever it was.

Luckily the old farmhouse north of Milburn had not been razed, only boarded up, and that so crudely Calla had no difficulty prying loose boards in order to crawl inside so when after the first time the girl disappeared from her great-aunt's house in Shaheen, no word or warning and seemingly amiable enough the hour before, working beside her aunt in the kitchen, perhaps in her rapt efficient somehow vacant-eyed way, the family knew where she had gone and how to locate her: a trek of about eight miles as the crow flies from the house in Shaheen to the house in the country, across fields both plowed and planted and unplowed and dense with wild rose treacherous as barbed wire, across creeks and gullies and glacier-gouged landscapes familiar to Calla Honeystone even by night *Oh I could have walked there in my sleep—I did walk there, more than once, in my sleep* as, though lacking any proprietary sense of home, home-owning, property, she was drawn by an almost physical yearning to a certain point of consciousness; a position fixed not only in space but in time from which, when her eyelids first fluttered open in the morning, she knew where she was. She slept on the filthy remains of a mattress in one of the upstairs bedrooms, she devoured fruit from the overgrown orchard, even raw field corn and potatoes and counted it no hardship, still less a disgrace, as her mother's people did.

So they came to bring her back home. Once, and another time, and yet another time, red-haired gaunt-faced Calla Honeystone silent and sullen in the back of a rattling horse-drawn wagon, gnawing at her knuckles until they bled, her skin livid with sunburn like shame and the odor lifting from her unwashed body a powerful stink as much earth as animal yet, light-headed with hunger, she associated this state of being with a state of purity of craving of infinite exalted desire, hardly listening as her relatives spoke to her in tones of worry, dismay, disgust, asking what was she doing to herself, was she crazy, did she want to be put into a county home?—*was* she a wild animal? (for no term of disapprobation was more extreme: to be called a wild animal was to be accused of lapsing from humanity itself, a humanity so recently and tenuously won) and brought back to Shaheen she was made to bathe, to eat, to dress like the others. She said, "Let me go—nobody would know if I lived out there, nobody would know or care," and they replied, "Yes but everyone would know, it would bring shame on us all," and she cried, her face heated as if slapped, "What do I care about shame: I don't care about shame!"

They perceived there was only one solution: to find a husband for Calla as quickly as possible.

11

And this task which might have seemed in theory a daunting one turned out to be unexpectedly easy: for Calla Honeystone at seventeen was a striking girl and in the company of strangers could be stirred, for duplicity's sake if for no other, to behave with a childlike yet sensuous charm; like a feral cat knowing instinctively in which direction advantage lay. Thus thinking as she considered the taciturn and seemingly shy, even abashed man proposed to her as a husband *I can keep my distance from that one!*

Despite her cleverness, Calla Honeystone knew little of marriage.

She knew by way of perception how and even why creatures were bound to reproduce themselves but her knowledge did not extend itself to a theory, let alone a principle, that might be applied to *her*.

George Freilicht was thirty-nine years old; a bachelor; not short, nor certainly stunted, but with a look of being undersized, as if his legs were cut off at the knee. His head was large and imposing, set, it seemed, crookedly on his narrow shoulders; his eyes were small and darkly shiny and brooding; inside his bristling yet drooping moustache his lips appeared miniature and bloodless, set over slightly protuberant rabbit teeth in a mimicry of a smile. An ugly little man—but ugly with character, distinction. On nearly every part of his solid body, as a wife would discover, there grew coarse wirelike hairs, graying, springy to the touch, of which the hairs on his head were but the exaggeration, the excess. Freilicht had inherited from his vigorous father a farm of over one hundred acres near Shaheen partly bordering the Chautauqua River; he was not his father, but was willing to work—to work himself and others—to assure a modicum of success, or at least to forestall failure; the creases in his face were marks of worry and weather, and his hands were a farmer's hands—the fingers broad and stubby, scarred, stained, battered, the nails thick as horn. What Calla Honeystone confidently mistook for shyness was a habitual parsimony regarding words, as if words, breath itself, were to be consciously economized. Even in a farming community of German immigrants and their descendants in which qualities of frugality were hardly uncommon George Freilicht was known as tightfisted and meanly scrupulous; it was said of him by his own relatives that the man possessed the pertinacity of a woodchuck, that most rapacious, cunning, and unkillable of wild creatures.

George Freilicht wanted to marry; or wanted eagerly to be married; or, if he neither wanted to marry nor to be married, he could no longer forestall the entreaties, the pleadings, the naggings, the importunings of his beloved mother and his numerous female relations, that he be married at last, and have children—sons. Before it was too late! Before something happened, and God Himself lost patience, and it was too late!

So Freilicht had been cajoled, even shamed, decidedly pushed into this meeting with—with precisely whom, he did not know, for he left such things to his mother and aunts and cousins, the sifting through of the available women (which were not many: not many, in any case, for George Freilicht of all men) in the Shaheen area; and though this girl with the astonishing red hair and yet more astonishing face was not a Lutheran she *was* a Methodist—a devout Christian, the Freilichts had been assured.

And now the girl, Miss Calla Honeystone, her hair neatly brushed and plaited, her eyes clear, and fingernails perfectly clean, smiled—smiled at *him*.

Did she, the doomed girl, imagine in him, that gnomish little man, an opportunity of a rare kind?—did she see in him an adult less intimidating than the other adults of her world, as he was, so certainly, less physically imposing?—did she see here a way out of her relatives' house in Shaheen that was not only legitimate but would be blessed, by God and by man?—or was her surge of confidence but a young girl's exulting in her own sexual power?—that mirage of sexual power?

In any case, Calla smiled. With the artlessness of a seductive child. Twined a strand of her wavy flamey hair around a forefinger, and smiled.

And though George Freilicht was too startled to smile in response something did soften about his prim pursed mouth; his coarse-pored skin livened in a blush; the angry little pulse at his temple relaxed. A smile from this young girl where another sort of response had been antici-pated was a candle lit impulsively in his heart: it would not burn for long but for the moment, astonishingly, there it was.

12

Only a few photographs survive of the woman who would be my mother's mother.

Family accounts have it, Calla ripped the rest to shreds.

One, badly discolored and dog-eared, shows the bride in a high-necked wedding dress, posed stiffly against a velvet backdrop; the date is November 11, 1907. The wedding dress with its conventionally full skirt is made of something shiny and sleek, like satin; the bodice is tight and lacy and the sleeves are long and tight too, cuffed at the wrists in lace. There is a bridal veil that floats like gossamer on the bride's fussily braided and coiled hair. Inside the glaringly white dress the bride, a mere girl, sits self-consciously, one might guess miserably; her body is lean, not very womanly, with high narrow shoulders, long thin arms, bones prominent at the wrists. The face is strong, oval-shaped, arguably beautiful, but shadowed with a sort of adolescent irony; the eyes too level and direct in their gaze at the camera. There is nothing maidenly or coy here, nothing prettily pleading *Do you like me? Do you like my dress, my face, my hair? You won't judge me harshly—will you?* The feet, long narrow boyish feet, are set flat in their white satin pumps and the knees beneath the satin skirt are a bit spread, as a man might sit; as if the bride is impatient to have her photograph taken, to leap to her feet and escape.

Another less formal photograph shows Calla standing at the rear of the Freilicht house, the backdrop now a grape arbor, overexposed in sunshine.

Here Calla is standing with her arms tightly crossed under her high, small, hard-looking breasts; Calla smiling with half her mouth, sullenly, or sadly, or perhaps indifferently, her gaze abstract and unfocussed. In this photograph Calla is obviously pregnant: still a young girl, grown tall for her bones, angular, awkward, but with a small round belly only partly disguised by the loose skirt of her plain dark dress. Though the photograph is blurry, as if seen through a medium dense and uncertain as time itself, her features are clear—her eyebrows heavy and brooding and darkly defined as if someone has shaded them in with pencil on the matte surface of the photograph. Calla's splendid hair is unbraided and lustrous, falling past her shoulders; she is standing solidly on her heels, legs slightly parted and knees bent, to balance the weight of her belly. No date on the back of the photograph except the terse "1908."

And so around me life took on the contour and texture of a dream, though I was not the dreamer.

13

Was Calla disappointed in her marriage?—not at all.

Too much pride for that.

Nor was she resentful, or embittered. Nor disgusted.

No emotion at all. No emotion regarding the marriage except to think *This is how aloneness is: this.*

No emotion regarding the husband; the ugly little doggy-eyed man covered in bristling grayish black hairs like wires, him with his clammy feet and toenails gnarled and discolored where they weren't in fact missing entirely, yes and his tobacco-stained teeth, and the wormy lips, the belly creases inside the woolly fur and the smell of his long winter underwear, the touch of it in the laundry, the soapy churning water never hot enough to get out the stains, the odor of his body, yes and his breath too as stale at midday as in the morning after a night of his heavy sweating panting sleep and the rattling breath and the grinding of his teeth groaning in his sleep twitching and flailing and his bare bony clammy feet and his flat nasal voice *Edith? Edith?* and the frown of perplexity between his eyes sharp as if she'd made it herself with a pen knife but no she felt no emotion for him, too much pride for that.

"Why should it matter?—when nothing matters."

These were words she said aloud. Speaking, if to anyone, to God.

Not in complaint either but as mere statement of fact *for of course God already knows, He is only waiting for us to catch up with His knowledge.*

The aloneness of the soul consoled Calla. And certain immutable facts: the crows gathering at dusk in the trees down behind the Freilicht house were the crows gathering at dusk in the trees behind the house of Calla's childhood: the same crows, the same surprising strength and agility in their black bodies, the same harsh inquisitive cries. And the rich smells of rot, of soil, of last year's leaves exposed in spring; the trickling of water in the April thaw; the dripping of icicles, the rivulets making their way down the windows, the ditches, the streams, the creeks making their way veinlike through the hilly countryside to the river, to the lake, the Great Lakes of which Calla had only heard and never seen. And the seeping of her secret blood in her loins. And its cessation: the swelling of her belly which no power of her fevered will could stop. *If this is a dream it is not my dream, for how should I know the language in which to dream it?*

14

The Freilichts did not know what to make of her, their George's young wife. They had thought they would like her, now they were not so sure. The mother, Anya Freilicht, was not so sure. For Calla could never remember to call her husband's mother "Mother": when she addressed the dwarfish little barrel-shaped woman, she called her "Mrs. Freilicht" as if thrusting away her own rightful name onto another. And Calla, standing tall, a full head taller than the old woman, rarely looked her in the face, at all.

Anya Freilicht had a flushed corroded face inside which a young girl's baffled and furious face was contained, and her eyes that were shrewd damply blinking little pig's eyes shone with the hurt of a young girl as well. "She thinks she is too good for me, that Edith of yours. Too good for us all," Mrs. Freilicht complained. "Where does she have the *right*—!"

Freilicht murmured words that sounded like, "She doesn't think that, Mother," but he was vague and ashamed, and hid his voice in his moustache, or in his teeth, behind his hand. He was new at all this—new at marriage, had not wanted it, not at all—as new as his bride and as disoriented by the preposterous combination of formality and intimacy that marriage provides, demands. Thus he refused to discuss his wife with any of the family, even his mother. Grinding his teeth he muttered, "Leave it be, Mother, for God's sake," turning aside so that the astonished woman could not quite hear, "—you know nothing of her, or me."

To Calla, who was "Edith," he spoke in the same voice, his fingers now fumbling in his moustache and his eyes averted, "—She asks only that you call her 'Mother.' And that you respect her. If you could try—."

Calla exclaimed in her bright glib voice, her eyes too averted, "Oh I do. Yes I *do*. Whenever I think of it I *do*."

So Freilicht fled the house. Fled to the barns even after dark, after supper. For a farmer with so many head of livestock there is always something to do, there is always more than can be humanly done. He fled to the fields. He hitched up the team in an April hailstorm and plowed fields, and plowed fields. He tramped about the marsh in thigh-high rubber boots, in the muck. He worked beside his hired men, not to spy on them as they naturally thought but, working beside them, to be one of them. He should not have married, but God so ordained. He should not, but—. And now—. He was a bachelor bred in the bone for celibacy and childlessness and he knew now the slow-dawning unspeakable horror that he had surrendered the supreme control of his near-forty years of life to something that could no more be controlled than it could be clearly defined. George Freilicht *had* now a wife; George Freilicht *was* now a husband. The fierce baffled passion he felt for the young red-haired woman who was obliged by marital law to share his bed was nothing of which he could speak to any human being, and that God Himself was a witness to this passion was a source of profound humiliation. He feared he would come in time to hate God too.

So thinking, one day, Freilicht injured his foot in an accident—yes, another toenail had to be picked out with a tweezers, in fragments, out of the bloody stub of a little toe and the pain was a tongue of flame sent by God to cleanse the sinner's soul for however brief a while. *Praise to You in Your infinite wisdom.*

15

In the early weeks of Calla's marriage the man who was her husband dared not touch her.

Though lying panting and stricken beside her touching himself in stealth when he believed her asleep—touching himself with a bachelor's sure swift pragmatic anguished precision as his young wife lay turned from him at the edge of the bed her hands shut into fists and her lower lip caught in her sharp teeth but her breathing rhythmic and placid thinking *How I loathe you, how I wish you were dead dead dead* dropping off to sleep against the grain of her obdurate will.

Then one day in the heat of midsummer Calla found herself with no premeditation, no preparation certainly, simply walking away; having completed a stint of housework under her mother-in-law's supervision, sweaty, her hair in damp ringlets, yet uncomplaining, for Calla Honeystone was never one to complain nor even to betray her innermost feelings *She isn't natural* the Freilicht women murmured among themselves—*she will never make a mother unless she changes,* and now that afternoon in the airless heat-haze there she was stealing away as if her feet had their own volition, their own instinct.

She returned to the old house north of Milburn of course.

Puzzled to see how dilapidated it was, and the out-buildings in even worse condition, everything shabby, weed-choked, roofs covered in a lurid green moss like mange, the floorboards sagging, broken; and every-where—had years passed?—many years?—the skeletons of birds and rodents underfoot, a little pile of them in a corner of the kitchen beneath the sink, and Calla's eyes filled with tears of hurt and outrage *If You abandon me why then I will abandon You: You and Your Only Begotten Son both* and she lay exhausted on the floor in the room upstairs that had once been hers, too tired and her head pounding too violently for her to mind the dirt, the dust, the cobwebs, the tiny perfect skeletons, the needle-sharp shafts of sun-shine that penetrated the walls and ceiling and would have blinded her had she stared at them for long. She lay down, she hugged her knees and gave herself up not to sleep but to death *Why then I will abandon You, I will never be his wife again* and this exalted state of being she associated with purity, with cleanliness, with virginity, she lay with her eyes shut tight frightened of hearing murmurous voices and the rattling of the horse-drawn wagon that meant they were coming for her coming to take her back home not to let her die here but to take her back home, and resolved as she was to stay awake that she might hear them and escape them, she fell into a dazzling sleep and dreamed that, yes, they were here, not only her Shaheen relatives but the man who was her husband, calling *Edith? Oh—Edith?* as one might call a sick person who was also dangerous, and even as she dreamed they were here to return her against her will to that other place, they came for her, and did.

16

Then there were the nights in sweating nightmare succession when husband and wife struggled wordless, seemingly nameless, in that bed, on that horsehair mattress near as hard as any floorboards. This grunting creature who fumbled at Calla's breasts, his clumsy stubby fingers on her belly, the anguish and heat of his breath that smelled, these nights, of alcohol, in shame and desperation he tried to force his knee—his knee that was so hairy! so laughingly hairy! like a gorilla's Calla had seen pictured in a magazine!—between her legs, yes but Calla was too quick for him, too strong, using her elbows and knees and fingernails and even her head for butting so that she was able to force him from her, triumphant. And wordless, each of them wordless. And covered in sweat, and panting.

So for some minutes the man lay still, his heart knocking so hard in his chest that Calla could feel the bed rock beneath them; the floor of the room rock; the very foundation of the old farmhouse; and in her mind's eye she could see the brass lightning rod on the highest peak of the highest roof gleaming with reflected moonlight and this, too, tremulous, quivering with the outrage of George Freilicht's heartbeat.

Then after some minutes the man would turn to her again, though hating her, and hating himself, silent, lips drawn back from his teeth in an arrested grimace, misery, loathing, duty, his disproportionate body damp and frizzed with hair, his muscles straining, and the terse hard rod between his legs tremulous, too, with outrage; so again they struggled wordless and grunting; and again with a surge of strength Calla managed to thrust the man from her; and this time he might give up abruptly for the night, as if released from his travail by an impersonal force or authority, his strength draining rapidly from him, and the rod between his legs immediately gone limp less in shame than in simple animal exhaustion so that he crawled from that place of combat and slept on the carpet so that at dawn Calla woke suddenly amidst the disheveled unspeakably fouled sheets to hear a man's labored wet-rasping breath that seemed to be coming at her from all sides of the twilit room as if he had already died and passed into the very air, like God Himself in Whom in fact Calla was ceasing to believe.

17

And then I weakened, and I died.
And my children were born.

Through the long summer Calla rejoiced in her tender bruised breasts and belly; the discolored flesh of her upper arms and muscular thighs; her backbone that ached from that grim nightly grappling: surveying herself with satisfaction, in secret, knowing that he, the despised husband, was mirrored to her, equally bruised and battered, yet truly humbled as Calla was not. *For she had her pride: always, Calla had her pride.* During the lengthy days, in their clothes, upright, adult, moving sanely among others, husband and wife maintained an air of decorum, courtesy, their eyes tactfully averted from each other and their voices unemphatic. If others watched them calculatingly—not only the ever-vigilant Mrs. Freilicht but the several Freilicht relatives who lived in the farmhouse with them, and others who came on Sundays to visit—they gave no indication of seeing. It was as if, by day, neither felt the need to acknowledge a connection with or responsibility for their fevered nocturnal selves. It was as if they had agreed that marital shame need not follow them across the threshold of the bedroom door.

Yet: if Calla were forced to pass close by Freilicht in some cramped space, on the steep narrow staircase for instance, she perceived how the poor man recoiled slightly from her, as if a charge of static electricity leapt between them; if she made an abrupt movement, even if only to set down a plate heaped with steaming food in front of him, she perceived how he shuddered and flinched, or managed to restrain himself from flinching. *Poor man! poor fool!* She knew, for all her studied obliviousness, that crude jokes were being made behind Freilicht's back, about his marriage; about the likelihood, or the unlikelihood, of his ever fathering any children. She knew how people glanced at her, and at him, thinking their lewd thoughts. How some frowned. How some dared smile. And after an accident during wheat harvesting when both Freilicht and another man were injured, though fortunate, as it was said, not to have suffered far worse in the blades of a threshing machine, Calla one midday regarded her husband down the length of the dining room table seeing his stiff graying hair, his creased forehead and cheeks like a much-wrinkled rag, his morose abashed gaze fixed upon her and those small bloodless lips, she saw the pity of him, the pathos, yet a certain kindliness too, a patience beyond all human endurance, and it occurred to her that though she did not love him in the slightest he was perhaps a good man: a man who deserved better than life gave him. So, unthinking, moved by her own impulsive magnanimity, Calla smiled. Feeling no love, no affection, and entirely ignorant of what such a smile might mean to him, from her, Calla smiled—revealing those strong white teeth that were chipped from childhood mishaps but very white, very strong, dazzling to Freilicht who stared at her as if unwilling to believe his eyes.

So I weakened, and I died. And my children pushed forward to be born.

18

Three babies in little more than three years.

A boy, another boy, a girl: and it began to be whispered that Edith Freilicht was not a natural mother, surely there was something wrong with her, how readily she allowed the care of her babies to fall into others' hands, how painful she found nursing them at the breast, and how clumsy, how strained, how vague her manner with them as if they presented to her, in all their mindless heated baby-flesh, the most incomprehensible of riddles. In wonderment she thought *I am drowning, that is what this is* but she felt no terror only a calm and almost logical tranquility as if the waters had risen over her head already and she had only to acknowledge them, and die. Always she had believed that the soul is alone before God: now she did not believe, much, in God. Or, if she believed in God, she had ceased to think of Him. She took solace in the impersonal life that flowed through her like an underground stream; subterranean, secret; the life that generated babies, and ate away voraciously at all organic life, and animated the wind in the trees, and made her heart beat, and beat and beat, without her consent or understanding. She had faith in that life that was unnamable and she thought with a sudden half-angry conviction *I am not drowning, really. I will swim free.*

Soon after Calla became pregnant with the third baby physical relations ceased forever between her and her husband: one night when, tentatively, he touched her, she moved his hand away; and when, another night, he touched her again, again she moved his hand away. And after the baby's birth Calla was ill for some time with an infection, and after her illness subsided there was no proper or inevitable time for Freilicht to touch her again, no moment when, smiling or otherwise, she invited him to do so, thus she had no need to tell him *No, no more* nor had her husband any need to slip from their bed hurt and humiliated and wounded in his masculine vanity.

He's as relieved as I, now he can be a bachelor again.

So Calla began to wander away from the house, as if absentmindedly; at first for an hour or two, then for longer and longer periods of time. Even in chill rainy weather she might disappear for most of a day without having troubled to tell anyone where she was going . . . sometimes in a place she'd never seen before, a birch woods, a hollow by a stream, an old long-abandoned cemetery in no-man's-land, in the ruins of an old settler's cabin, she was overcome by the need to lie down and sleep so that she had no choice but to lie down like an animal overtaken by sleep having time only to assure that she was hidden from view *And how different, in such places, than the sleep of routine and dull domesticity, in a bed, in a room, in a house, within walls shared by others* in that profound sleep that carried her so far she woke restored to herself yet at the same time amnesiac, unable to recall for some minutes where she was, or who she was, or why, or how.

Naturally, the first few times, the Freilichts searched for Calla. But if they saw her it was never in one of her secret places, and never curled up defenseless and asleep: only on her way home, walking along the lane or through a corn-stubbled field, her clothes soiled and untidy, burrs and leaves in her matted hair, face slightly puffy with the balm of unfettered sleep. And the woman would have the audacity to lift a hand in greeting as if she were surprised, delighted at seeing them so unexpectedly: "Oh—what are you doing *here?*"

19

How strange she was. How . . . strange.

A beautiful young woman so innocent of vanity (or was it self-respect) she scarcely cared how she dressed, even on Sundays; even when company came; like a female derelict sometimes forgetting to wash her hair from one week to the next so that its wavy-red luster turned opaque and there lifted from her a faint warm rank animal smell. Mrs. Freilicht, who chided Calla about so many things, chided her about this. And this, and *this*. Why for instance did Calla wear clothes already soiled?—stockings already frayed?—her worst gloves, her shabbiest hat? Why bring in for a bouquet on the dining room table a disorderly handful of those wildflowers—chicory, asters—that would begin to droop and fall within a few hours? *And why was she so loath to look in a mirror?*

Once, asked about the mirror, Calla laughed and said,
"—But there's nobody *there*."

She talked in riddles, sometimes. Mrs. Freilicht
objected.

What a daughter-in-law: with a habit of murmuring
to herself words you couldn't hear; humming, whistling,
singing under her breath—"The Old Rugged Cross" and
"Jesus Loves Me This I Know" were her favorite hymns,
sung repeatedly in an uninflected deep contralto voice too
pure, really, to be her own. And with a habit, too, more
disconcerting yet, of lapsing into long spells of silence
during which she seemed to hear very little that was said
to her, though she pretended otherwise. And there was the
time when, working one day in the kitchen, Mrs. Freilicht
supervising the preparation of a mammoth Sunday dinner
to which relatives from upriver were invited, her
daughter-in-law dared interrupt her conversation with a
cautionary tug of her wrist, saying, "Shhhh!" and Mrs.
Freilicht asked, startled, "Ja?—what is it?" There was the
girl standing frozen in the middle of the floor, her head
flung back and her jaws rigid, her eyes fixed on something
that might have been floating in a corner of the kitchen;
and after a long worrisome pause she whispered, "—I was
only trying for us two to not be wakened, Mrs. Freilicht.
If we've been dreaming."

Calla made an effort, they could see how, against the
grain of her nature, she made the effort, repeatedly, with
her faint wondering smile and perplexed eyes, to be a
mother to her children—a good and attentive and loving

"mother" to these three small children. How could it be said that she was "cold," "unfeeling," "unnatural"—a "bad" mother? Yet the truth was, when Calla was not in the room with her children she tended to forget them.

From the first, much of the care of the babies had fallen to others—the indefatigable mother-in-law primarily, but one or another female relation besides; for always in such farm families there were women not only willing but grateful to take care of babies, lacking their own or having seen their own grow up too swiftly, and these women tended to Calla's babies when she was unwell, or distracted, or absent. And what perverse pleasure in the arrangement: that Mrs. Freilicht had the satisfaction of tending to her grandchildren as well as the satisfaction of complaining bitterly of the children's mother.

"She is not right. She does not even look at them *right*."

But Freilicht, who might have said that after all he had not wanted to marry, and had not chosen his wife, refused to discuss these matters. What God had ordained, God had ordained: he would not die childless after all; he had not one but two sons. Only to Calla, once, did this taciturn and abashed man bring up the subject of their children, when, after an Easter Sunday spent at a cousin's upriver farm Calla's seeming indifference to her children had provoked comment, and Calla responded, unthinking, immediate, with the air of a child who cannot be relied upon not to speak the obvious, "Oh—but I didn't really want them, I thought *you* did."

For a moment Freilicht stared at her, this woman, the

mother of his children, *his* children, *his* wife, and could not speak.

His skin was weather coarsened, his small pale lips were quivering, speechless. And that angry little worm-like pulse in his temple beginning visibly to beat.

And his hands: those blunt scarred fingers closed themselves into fists, quivering too. This Calla saw, and recognized the sign, but did not step back from him.

Quietly she said, "—You could divorce me. It's done. Send me away. You don't need me, the children don't need me. Let me go away. Don't let anyone bring me back."

Freilicht composed himself. He managed even to laugh.

"Don't be ridiculous, Edith," he said, "—you're my wife: you aren't going anywhere."

Never once in the several years of their marriage had George Freilicht called her Calla, she'd never revealed to him her true name.

20

When I first laid eyes on him it was in innocence for how could I know it was him!

She had been walking, and walking quickly, with no mind for where she was taken. How many miles, and in which direction. It was a warm autumn shimmering with bees. High overhead dense compacted grayish white clouds blew about the sky, the sky was hot with sun, so bright it had no color.

The creek drew her, a nameless creek somewhere east of Shaheen, wide, low, murmurous, with a dank smell, the smell of lichen dried and baked on flat white boulders, the smell of dead fish, a creek that would deepen and begin to move more swiftly, with more purpose and urgency, as it approached the Chautauqua River, snaking through hills lush with vegetation, junglelike, immense willow trees hanging over the water as if crouching and Calla was smelling something rich and fecund and sweetly intoxicating that drew her too: made her smile, and drew her: the apple rot, the fermentation of a compost dump behind an old ruin of a cider mill, the weatherworn boards and steep broken roof and the crude crumbling stone foundation familiar to her or to her mind's eye: *I have been here before.* But the place was no puzzle to her, nor was when she'd seen it previously. Calla's mind was too restless for such speculation.

A low humming-buzzing as of people talking talking talking just out of earshot. She shaded her eyes and saw that it was bees, wasps, flies—amazing clouds of them, glittering imbricated clouds of them above the small mountain of apple compost behind the mill sloping not only to the bank of the creek but into the creek as in an old catastrophe. Above her the cider mill rose hulking and utterly still, though about it the world was buzzing, shimmering, alive.

Calla saw that a man was fishing off the creek bank: a stranger, seemingly: squatting on his heels at the edge of the slow-moving creek, his back to her. She was standing by one of the empty mill windows, looking into a corner of the mill and through another empty window ribbed with broken glass and cobwebs, and attentively she stood on her toes watching this solitary fisherman, oddly dressed for fishing in the backcountry in a new-looking straw hat and a tight-fitting black coat or jacket with a preacherly look to it, surely too warm for this September day, and wasn't there something unusual about the man? something about his dark dark skin, his profile? that held Calla fascinated, and cautious, wary of being seen yet reluctant to move away. She was not by nature a woman given to small nervous fears but she had known since childhood to avoid men, even men whose faces and names she might recognize, in such settings. No man had ever laid a hand on her in her wanderings but a few, a very few, had tried, and Calla did not want to invite misunderstanding here *He's a black man—a Negro* standing as she was so avidly watching, staring, feeling that stab of advantage we feel when we see someone who not only does not see us but has no sense of us entirely. Calla was holding herself on the window ledge, strong enough to balance herself there on her elbows and forearms, not minding how the stone ledge littered with bits of glass and debris hurt her bare flesh, perhaps the odor of sweet apple rot had gone to her head, sweetly befuddling.

In her soft sinuous contralto Calla called, "Hello!"— too far from the creek for the fisherman to hear her, and again, "—Hello! Someone else is here too!" and now the fisherman lifted his head, turned to look around perplexed, but seeing nothing and no one returned to his fishing line, to the creek that from Calla's angle of vision on higher ground was a broad flat ribbon of light laid down between banks choked with vegetation as in a time so ancient not a one of those living things had a name.

So minutes passed. How many, Calla would not have known.

Calla took delight in observing the stranger, the black man, from her strategic position; bracing herself on the windowsill, her muscles small but hard, strong, bearing her up. In giving birth she had three times bled, and bled, and bled, until that final time she had believed they meant to allow her to bleed to death once the baby was wrenched from her, their baby, and not hers, yet she'd held stubbornly on to the thin stream of life as if with her very fingers, yes she'd held on tight, tight and stubborn, she'd lived and now months later she'd recovered completely from the anguish and ignominy, the unspeakable insult of it, now she was restored to herself again, her body lank yet hard with muscle, ungiving. When hours later or in the morning she returned to the Freilichts it would be bearing her mother-in-law a face masklike with grime, hair wild and tangled, exposed skin stippled with insect bites and scratches and the woman would stare at her with those outraged baffled eyes but not ask her, for she would not stoop, as she claimed, to ask this question another time, where Calla had been: *I do what I do, what I do is what I wanted to have done.*

It seemed Calla's speech was teased out of her by the humming of the insects, the placid glitter of their tiny light-bearing bodies above the sliding heaps of rot, and there was the old mill, too, in its dreamlike dilapidation as if its sliding had been arrested, halted, in the very moment of motion, and the creek with no name she could recall, yes and the tall black fisherman in the straw hat and snug-fitting jacket now standing alert and quizzical as if preparing to smile, readying himself to be teased and coaxed again by Calla Honeystone leaning there on the window ledge just out of the fiercest shaft of sun, saying, "—Hello! You! Don't you know someone else is here too!"

But the fisherman could not see her. Tall and attentive and shading his eyes, face plaited in wonder, he could not see her, though he seemed to be looking directly at her. And if he heard her voice he did not hear her words. And if he heard her voice he did not believe it any human voice, thus did not investigate any further, though he did remain standing there on the bank his fishing line forgotten behind him until at last Calla lowered herself to the ground, slipped away almost repentant and released him.

21

It was 1911, in the Chautauqua River Valley.
Aloud Calla said, as if tasting the word, "Ne-gro."
And black and rich and strange it tasted, like licorice.

For Calla was after all a country girl, rawboned and inexperienced and young for her age, who despite her curiosity and boldness knew little of the world. Never once had she seen a black man or a black woman close up, rarely in fact had she seen blacks save in photographs or drawings and from time to time on the street in the small river city of Derby where the Freilichts shopped on Saturdays occasionally and where Calla managed to slip away from the others to explore afoot the unfamiliar fascinating streets, making her way with less assurance than she did in the country but drawn by the evidence of her eye, these commercial buildings rising five and six and even seven stories above Main Street, these elegant brick houses on High Street, and there were livery stables, and hotels, and a railroad depot, and a granary, and churches and brickyards and open markets but the main thing was people: numberless people: strangers who knew neither her nor her name and if they glanced at her at all (which naturally they did: this tall forthright red-haired young woman who carried herself even in her heavy unstylish skirts like a man) had not the slightest idea where she was from, to whom in all practical terms she belonged.

And among these strangers there were sometimes blacks: Negroes: descendants of slaves, Calla knew; most of them only recently emigrated up from the South.

In Derby, those Saturdays, Calla slipped away from the Freilichts and walked for hours. Beyond the railroad depot and the railroad yards, along the riverfront, the barges, the tugs, the horse-drawn vehicles, and the slaughterhouses where the air pulsed with heat, blood, excrement, death, and it was animal terror she smelled, her nostrils wide with it, her own blood quickened. Where no white woman would walk but she was unfrightened and unembarrassed staring, staring hard, and in the hollow of Negro row houses and shanties, close by the rear of one of the slaughterhouses, across a makeshift bridge spanning a drainage ditch where the brackish water was threaded with rust she was stared at in return, sometimes defiantly, sometimes with blank amazement and wonder, and she would have smiled and lifted a hand in greeting except she knew she had not the right: in their eyes she was a white woman, one of the enemy.

She felt a thrill of horror, amid the blacks. That their immediate ancestors had been *owned*. Not these blacks as individuals for most of them were young, many were children, but their blackness, their essence—that had been *owned*. And now in this city amid the heterogeneous white population of the city they were so relatively few in number—like small dark carp in an immense school of fiercely golden carp, depending upon God knows what precarious law or whim of nature to survive. *Like me they are outcasts in this country. No not like me: they are true outcasts.*

22

Calla's little girl Emmaline was so sick with measles, ice packs could bring her fever down only a degree or two and it hovered meanly at 101 degrees Fahrenheit while the child lay eerily still and uncomplaining,

her eyes closed, yet not entirely closed, and Calla paced
about the room striking the palms of her hands together as
Mrs. Freilicht and one of Calla's sisters-in-law fussed and
scolded and worried together, and suddenly—this was a
windy sunswept morning, April 1912, Freilicht was not at
home—Calla's attention was drawn to an unexpected sight
out the window: there alongside the house was a man, a
stranger: dressed with seeming formality in a preacherly
black suit and a black bowler hat and what was he doing
there? what was he holding in his hands?—walking slow
as a sleepwalker as if measuring something on the ground
with his eyes, Calla could see a double-pronged instru-
ment of some kind he was holding at about chest level, and
staring down at him, moving along the window as he
moved below then going to another window to watch,
Calla began to breathe more quickly, staring, seeing the
man's skin stained dark as wood with a purplish red sheen
in the bright sunshine, thinking *It's him, of course it's him.*

Without a word of explanation to the women who
stared at her speechless, nor even a fleeting backward
glance at the feverish child in the bed, Calla ran downstairs, heels pounding hard on the stairs and then outdoors
into the bright windy day, not taking time even to snatch
up a coat or a jacket off the row of pegs by the kitchen door,
no time for such prudence: there she was, George Freilicht's very wife and the mother of his three small children
daring to run up breathless to a stranger, a Negro, trespassing on her husband's property: demanding who he
was? what was he doing? and the black man stared at her
for a beat or two before replying, as if whatever he might
reasonably have expected, trespassing on a white farmer's

property so blatantly, or so hopefully, it surely was not *this*—the black man stared at her and tipped his hat at her saying politely, "My name is Tyrell Thompson, ma'am, from a ways east of here, by trade I am a water dowser and I been happening to hear there's some farms around here that—" and Calla saw it *was* a dowsing rod the man held in his hands, a two-branched willow limb of about eighteen inches in length held chest-high like an oversized turkey wishbone, and she laughed, and the color came up in her face, and she said, "So that's it!"

In this way, Calla met Tyrell Thompson.

Or so it was afterward recounted.

Quickly, as if to forestall embarrassment, Tyrell Thompson explained to Calla that he had not exactly been invited to dowse for water but since he was passing through the valley and he'd been hearing that the water table was low, maybe even he'd happened to hear that the gentleman who owned this property was planning to drill for a new well, yes he was certain he'd heard that mentioned in Shaheen, he'd thought he would make a visit to offer his services gratis— "Like my daddy before me and his daddy before him I never charge any fee for the finding of water, ma'am, it's a sacred calling and must not be profaned, but should I find water, good fresh clear spring-water, and should the gentleman for whom I find it be pleased, I am not averse to accepting—" he paused, knitting his smooth high forehead as he searched for the proper word, "—a gift." Tyrell Thompson's voice was velvety soft, his diction formal. Calla smiled so hard her face ached and said as if she hadn't heard a word, "Yes I'm—Calla, I'm Mr. Freilicht's wife," quickly adding, laughing again, as a ragged-looking blush rose into her cheeks, "I mean—I live here."

Tyrell Thompson hesitated for the smallest fraction of an instant: then shook Calla's hand.

It was a formal, rather hurried gesture. No sooner had he shaken the woman's hand and felt the strength of her long slender fingers than he let it go.

Calla said, "Oh I think we've met before—us two."

Tyrell Thompson said, "Have—?"

Calla said, "Oh—you wouldn't remember, that's all."

Tyrell Thompson regarded Calla in mild indignation that she might be taunting him, or something more cruel. He said, with a little mock bow, gravely, "—Yes, ma'am, but I naturally would remember, you know that, ma'am."

Calla's blush deepened. As if they'd been quarreling she said, "My name is Calla—didn't you hear?"

Now Tyrell Thompson stared at Calla frankly perplexed.

Not knowing what to make of her and fearful of her, Tyrell Thompson the itinerant water dowser who was well over six feet in height and two hundred pounds in weight, by his own estimate thirty years in age, and built strong and husky and unmarked by life as a young bull except for trifling scar tissue above his eyes and here and there on his body and a rope burn inflamed like a rash on his neck and that old injury in his right knee that plagued him in damp weather and a filagree mark lengthwise on his broad back only a practiced eye would identify as a scar made by barbed wire—not knowing what to make of her Tyrell

Thompson bared his teeth in a smile that surprised him, one of those smiles like blows that fall upon us unaware, and said, "—Calla."

Tall as she was, Calla had to look up to look Tyrell Thompson full in the face, an angle and a posture to which she was unaccustomed. For a moment she felt vertigo as if the sky were tilting.

So that windy April morning as Emmaline lay in her fever doze on the second floor of the old farmhouse, her small body motionless beneath the covers, her eyes showing mucous crescents beneath her reddened lids, Calla and the Negro water dowser Tyrell Thompson were to be observed, and indeed were observed scrupulously and incredulously, making their way with slow deliberate steps about the house, the one in his tight-fitting black suit and black bowler hat holding the dowsing rod delicately in front of him and the other avidly watching and talking, talking animatedly—but what did George Freilicht's wife who was so silent within her household, so maddeningly vacant-eyed and strained in her smiles find to talk about with *him?*—that big burly dangerous-looking colored man?—why did those two smile at each other, at first shyly and fleetingly, then with more boldness, and why was their joined laughter so staccato and breathless, with a sound of shattering glass—which the women inside the house heard clearly in their imagining if not in their ears?

True: the water table on Freilicht's property had been gradually sinking for years, the previous summer he'd had to pay to have drinking water hauled from town but it had not been declared that George Freilicht intended to drill a new well, frugal as the man was, and cautious about spending money until there was no recourse but to spend it, thus how had the Negro water dowser known to come out here, unbidden?—and why had he come at a time when the owner of the farm was not home? All the years of her remembered life, a life now spanning beyond seven decades, Mrs. Freilicht had been unswerving and certain *You can't trust colored ever—except maybe if you know them by first and last names both and who their families are and who they work for and where they live and even then you can't trust them behind your back, you'd be a God-forsaken fool if you did* and now there was her George's wife cavorting and prancing out there for anyone to see in the company of—

"How can she! Like a common slut! Our Edith!"

Now a bit of time had passed, Calla and the water dowser Tyrell Thompson were more at ease with each other: Calla chattering away telling Tyrell Thompson things she hadn't ever told anyone and wouldn't ever have thought of telling, such as when she'd been a little girl a water dowser had come by her father's farm to locate water for a well and yes he'd found it and afterward she'd played trying to work a dowsing rod for herself but without success, the willow branch just stayed fixed in one position unless on purpose she made it move which was cheating so she wondered was water dowsing a gift you had to be born with or was it a skill to be acquired by practice and good intentions and Tyrell Thompson told her it was both, so far as he knew—"A human being is born with a gift for water like for singing or dancing or preaching or fighting but then it's God's will you refine it. That means discipline, and hard work, and a right way of thinking so that what is sacred is not cast down in the mud."

Tyrell Thompson explained that any sacred calling was profaned in the marketplace of a country like the United States or even if displayed for vanity's sake, yet there comes a time in a man's life when he may have to humble himself and risk profanation since the majority of God's progeny can't be lilies of the field, toiling not, yet being nourished and protected by the lifelong labor of others who spend their lives cutting away at the weeds choking the lilies' roots, so long as the laborer is properly humbled in his pride and is worthy of his hire God should not judge harshly, some say it is even His will, as in dowsing for water for instance where fresh clear spring-water is discovered in earth, in mud, in muck, in the very place of filth, to be drawn up for the benefit and glory of mankind. He explained that being able to detect water as he did—not smelling it exactly but somehow knowing it's there, "As it's said, 'like calls out to like'"—in truth he would not require an actual dowsing rod but that was how it had always been done, how he'd learned from his daddy and his daddy had learned from *his,* going back to the first water dowser who lived, it was like say you're a blind man drawn to sound no one else could hear, but he, Tyrell Thompson, believed in using the willow branch as a visible sign others could see and identify, and touch.

As Tyrell Thompson spoke—and his speaking was like singing with no music, yet paced to the subtle rhythms of music—he continued to walk with the dowsing rod held at chest level, so delicately, Calla was fascinated. She saw that his fingers were nearly twice the size of hers. A dark dark brown on the outsides, with a purplish red sheen beneath like fine wood many-layered in shellac, and on the insides a tender-looking pale pink, flushed and pink as her own, so a stab of feeling ran through her, and she said, "*Can* I touch it, then?—try it myself?" indicating the dowsing rod with a forefinger; and Tyrell Thompson frowned and said, "—When it's time."

If the man was having difficulty locating water on Freilicht's property he kept his difficulty to himself, never gave any indication of doubt. One of the clear facts about Tyrell Thompson.

Another was: he had faith.

It was not, yet it surely seemed, a deliberate taunting of those several pairs of eyes inside the Freilicht house, that Calla and the black man never remained in sight more than a few minutes but continued to circle the house in widening concentric rings; vanishing for bits of time altogether; so that eyewitnesses to the spectacle were forced to re-negotiate their positions, window to window, room to room. Mrs. Freilicht and one or another of George's sisters or aunts or cousins were speechless with wonderment and revulsion that that woman who held herself so proud in their company who shrank from being touched even by her own children was now walking so close by this stranger it seemed she brushed the sleeve of her dress against the sleeve of his coat, even once or twice blundered into him when he paused to regrip and refocus the dowsing rod *How dare she: like common white trash: like a slut: and that nigger black as sin like he'd climbed up out of the ground*

exactly the kind to slice your throat without asking any questions,
yes and then he'd wipe the knife on your clothes when he was
finished until by teasing degrees they moved, now a seeming couple, farther and farther from the house, farther
from those pairs of aghast eyes, down beyond the kitchen
garden that was a tangle of dead vines and plants and
lopsided bean poles from the previous year, and the grape
arbor, and the present well which was an ordinary stone-
and-concrete well (that if you leaned into cupping your
hands to your mouth and calling out you would hear an
echo immediate yet seeming to come from the bowels of
the earth, a hollow sonorous sound having nothing to do
with you in daylight standing with your feet flat and solid
on the surface of the earth), until at last they came to a wide
shallow grassy space bordering a pasture where in that
harsh morning sunshine white-faced cattle browsed placid
and motionless as painted cattle: and here Tyrell Thompson snorted "Huhhhh!" as unmistakably the willow
branch squirmed, and jerked, and the prong pointed
down.

"Here. Here's water. Right where we are standing."

Though truly Calla did not disbelieve, she'd seen it
herself, she insisted upon taking the branch from Tyrell
Thompson, and held it erect herself in wishbone position,
and again it squirmed and jerked in her fingers and the
prong pointed down—"Oh it's alive like a snake!" she
cried.

Tyrell Thompson said, modestly, "It *is* alive. Like we
are alive. And the water too—'like calls out to like.'"

Tyrell Thompson located a sizable rock to lay on the

grass marking the spot beneath which water was to be found.

Calla observed him gravely. By this time her hair was wind whipped and her lips blue with cold, the tips of her fingers like ice yet she never felt it, not a bit of discomfort, so rapt an attention did she give Tyrell Thompson. Expressing a wifely doubt she did not truly feel, she said, as Tyrell Thompson prepared to leave, "—But if he goes to all the trouble and expense of—of drilling—and if—if there's no water—"

Tyrell Thompson tipped the rim of his smart bowler hat with a flicker of impatience, and said, "Mrs. Freilicht, ma'am, my word is as good as my life."

So Calla stood silenced and corrected.

By morning of the following day, who knows how such things spread, word was everywhere in the valley that George Freilicht's wife, one of those impoverished Honeystones from up around Milburn, had hired a Negro, a stranger, against her husband's wishes, not simply to dowse for water on Freilicht's property but to drill for a new well. And more.

23

Though Calla was guiltless at the start, relations between her and Freilicht were altered forever: and in that grassy hollow by the pasture Tyrell Thompson's rock remained untouched for weeks, months. Freilicht saw it frequently but chose not to speak of it. To haul it away would be to acknowledge it, thus he did not haul it away, nor ask that one or another of his farmhands do so. Or maybe in fact he did not see it?

The Freilicht property, acquired in the mid-1800s along the south shore of the Chautauqua River, its considerable acreage, and the several barns, and the red-brick house, and the livestock, and the farming equipment, and numberless possessions under the roof of the house, were George Freilicht's: thus he had the privilege of seeing what he wished to see, and no more.

And of hearing what he wished to hear, and no more.

Each time Calla dared bring up the subject of a new well Freilicht said coldly that so long as there was water in the present well they could hang on a little longer. Calla persisted, "At least we must pay him. We owe him—" but she could not think what sum of money might be appropriate: twenty-five dollars, seventy-five dollars, one hundred dollars? Or only five dollars?—for Calla rarely handled money and rarely gave it a thought. "But it can only be a gift, it can't be direct," she said. "A water dowser of Tyrell Thompson's quality can't accept money for his services outright."

Freilicht said, "Oh can't he!"

Freilicht said, his voice rising, "*You* might owe him, *I* don't: if that nigger sets foot on my property again I'll shoot him down like a dog."

Rainfall during the summer was light and intermittent and by late August and early September there were lengthy rainless stretches and a heat wave of two weeks' duration when the cloudless bleached-blue sky gave off blinding heat from all directions and the daytime temperature climbed beyond 100 degrees Fahrenheit and by night rarely dropped below 80 degrees Fahrenheit and the creeks and water holes began to shrink and the river turned mud color revealing gouged-looking banks disfigured with the exposed roots of trees like astonished veins or nerves . . . and the husks of dead insects gathered underfoot, even inside the Freilicht house; and leaves curled, and browned, and fell from the trees; and the well required ever more pumping to yield its increasingly tepid, rust-specked water.

By mid-September the water table had dropped so low that Freilicht was again obliged to haul in water; yet still stubbornly the man resisted, awaiting rain, ever certain that God would not humiliate him and fail to send rain . . . though when rain did come in scattered explosive showers it was not sufficient to replenish his well. By this time Calla no longer spoke of water and the water dowser and what might or might not be owed the man, Calla was rarely present to speak to Freilicht at all, but others in the family begged him, Mrs. Freilicht herself begged him, so finally in late September Freilicht gave in and arranged for a Yewville company to drill a new well on his property by which time Tyrell Thompson's marker had mysteriously disappeared so when at last a new well was dug after five or six fruitless exploratory drillings there was no way of knowing or demonstrating that Tyrell Thompson had been the one to first discover the ideal site there in the grassy hollow by the pasture where thirty-six feet below the surface of the earth beyond loamy pebbly soil and serrated sheets of shale an underground stream flowed miraculously bright, sparkling, plenteous, with a taste pure as ice crystals on the tongue, and so cold it felt like fire.

And by that time, too, rumors had begun to spread through the valley about Calla and Tyrell Thompson, surely untrue, that the two were seen together hurrying in stealth, on country roads in the Shaheen area, in Tintern Falls, in the city of Derby, a tall beautiful red-haired white woman *he never should have married, that poor fool* and her black lover who was in some versions a water dowser clad in black near seven feet tall with a glass eye and a bad limp, in other versions a preacher with a scarred face and rope burns showing on his neck where he'd been hanged and left for dead *or maybe he's got nine lives, did actually come back from the dead vowing revenge* and in others a "rogue" of a Negro escaped from a chain gang in Georgia *come North to seduce white men's wives and take his pleasure and his revenge in one.*

PART
II

24

And when her life was split irrevocably in two
though not in half she would recall that night,
those nights when it did seem at least at the first that the
dream that contained her was a dream of her own deepest
purest most passionate wish and not a dream beyond her
control or comprehension, those nights that were a single
night *At first there was no moon, then like an eye opening there
was a moon almost blinding* and the man who was her
husband slept his heavy sullen wetly rasping perspiring
sleep seemingly unknowing and unsuspecting and Calla
slipped out from beneath the suffocating covers, not
needing to breathe, not needing to see in the familiar dark,
but how her heart beat! her pulse wild to leap in her wrist!
for she had heard him call for her *Calla oh Calla! Calla!* and
she could not deny him.

She had not in fact denied him, other times. And by
crude blunt brash daylight.

I do what I do: what I have done is what I have wanted to do
taking up her clothes where she'd carelessly laid them,
moving silently, barefoot and eager on her toes, and it's as
if she is sleepwalking, with such uncharacteristic grace and

caution her feet scarcely touch the floor, she dresses in an alcove of the upstairs hall swiftly bunching her hair up in a knot at the nape of her neck hearing him cry *Calla! oh Calla!* his voice light and mournful-sounding as the loons on the river that keep her awake these late-summer nights, her heart beating rapid as pain with desire with what she had not known was desire, and now she stands at the window seeing how, like hoarfrost, reflected light lies on the roof below her, and on the high-peaked roofs of the outbuildings, and on the conical metal roof of the silo, her eyes dilated now, almost entirely pupil, and it's impossible to determine in the moonlight in this world so drained of normal color where grass leaves off and earth begins; where earth leaves off and sky begins; where in the wind-rippled shadow of the hay barn Tyrell Thompson in his black clothes stands beckoning to her.

Calla oh Calla!

That name she'd taught him. Taught him to say. And each time he'd faltered shying from it out of habit murmuring *ma'am* or worse yet to her ears *Mrs. Freilicht,* she'd snatched up his hand in hers and squeezed the fingers hard digging in her nails so he laughed and winced *My name is Calla: Calla is my only name,* her face bright and fierce with what she hadn't known was desire, the terrible pulse of it, the hunger.

Now she is making her way down the narrow stairs at the rear of the house, those stairs pitched at a treacherous angle, steeper by night they seem than by day, and the youngest child Emmaline wakes in her sleep on the floor above open-eyed suddenly and terrified hearing the wind in the eaves, the wind blowing the clouds across the sky, there's the sound of a door being opened downstairs at the rear of the house, the sound of something slammed in the wind but heedless Calla is running across the wide moonlit space to the shadow of the barn where her lover Tyrell Thompson is waiting for her, thinking *It's true there is no shame in me: only hunger* and wordless he catches her in his arms strong enough to lift her in the crook of one arm and they embrace, they kiss, there's a kind of anger in their kissing, wanting to hurt *I love love love you* Calla wrapping her arms around the man, yes and her muscular legs too, fitting herself to him so he draws back his head laughing in mock alarm *Calla you going to be the death of me.*

They have to flee, they can't remain here, there's a dog barking and that man in the house if he wakes from his heavy sullen sleep has a shotgun, both barrels loaded, and laughing they make their way along the lane, their feet barely skimming the earth, arms around each other's waist they are running past the dessicated cornstalks shivering in the wind and past the marshy land where mosquitoes stir warmed by the scent of their blood and on the far side of the marsh there are birds singing faint and sweetly tentative as if it's morning—morning already—but the moon is still shining overhead *I was drawn after that man like water sucked by wind, shaping my shape to his* and it was true, in his arms in one of their snug hiding places in a no-man's-land by the river Calla screamed and screamed and screamed, wept, sobbed herself to sleep shaped to his shape curled like a baby waiting to be born like the lost memory of one of Calla's own babies snug and hot tight up inside her waiting to be born.

25

Most nights, there was a moon.

Or those nights recalled as if the doomed ferocity of certain emotions *I love only you God damn you I want only you, I'm no more a coward than you are* had been imparted to the night itself, the very sky that drew them out with a promise of giving shelter.

26

. . . lying there on the hearth by the fireplace downstairs in the musty parlor in a state between sleep and wakefulness warming herself with a little fire she'd built in haste but the birch wood seemed to be damp, gave off a warmth meager and grudging and the smoke made her cough behind her knuckles and her eyes water as if with hurt or grief *Calla oh Calla!* and now she was sprawled there shivering slattern her long snarled hair fanned out on her shoulders to dry, wavy red hair stippled with twigs, burrs, cobwebs, her hair needed washing, her face and her hands needed washing, there she was lying on the floor where no normal or sober or self-respecting woman would lie, her clothes looking as if slept in, the skirt mud stained . . . yes and her frayed stockings were wet and muddy, she'd kicked her ruined shoes off *from tramping about in the muck like a madwoman, you'd think her husband or his people would put a stop to it for very shame* neither asleep nor entirely awake half-sensing she was in danger but her eyelids were heavy, hair luxuriant fanned on her shoulders so the very sight of it, of her, that puffy slumberous look to her face would madden him, it was very early in the morning, just dawn, and sunless, a chill wan grudging light barely penetrating the lace curtains hanging from the parlor windows year after year prim and functionless save to accumulate by slow degrees that thin near-invisible film of dust that must then be laundered out of them, so carefully, by hand, gentle soap and no agitation and hung to dry out of the sun to prevent yellowing and shrinking and Calla might have been thinking how the rawboned young girl who had wandered the back roads and woods and fields and creeks was dead, now she was a mature woman, breasts, belly, thighs, loins, yes and even her face showing it, the eyes pinched at their corners, the mouth fleshy, puffy, much kissed, knowing, and Calla wiped roughly at her eyes with the back of her hand and happened then to see Freilicht standing there in the parlor doorway with the shotgun in his arms, certainly it was the shotgun but in that instant Calla had no clear thought *It's a gun, I'm going to die* seeing Freilicht's face as he advanced upon her grimacing, the eyes shining with conviction, glassily drunk, or beyond drunkenness, the jaws stubbled with gray-glinting wires, he was a man unfamiliar to her, ravaged and triumphant weaving drunkenly toward her having been drinking much of the previous day despite the family's pleas for him to stop, and through the long night, locked upstairs in that bedroom alternately praying on his knees and drinking whiskey waiting for the woman who was his wife to come back, so he had by this hour the look of a man drowned and hauled out of the water in mad triumph revivifying in air saying softly, "—You whore! *Whore!*" striking Calla in the face with his fist clumsy and off balance so he nearly fell on top of her, a second blow missed but her nose was spurting blood as she scrambled on her hands and knees rising to fight him, he struck her again and she clutched at his wrist, the shotgun was an impediment to them both as Freilicht sobbed and cursed her and Calla in grim silence struggled knowing it was her life *I can't die, not like this, it isn't time* as upstairs in their beds the children lay wakened and terrified hearing what they could not know yet understood were the sounds of struggle, that single raised despairing voice they could not know yet understood was their father's voice, and Calla snatched up the fire tongs, Calla crouched, panting, the tongs raised, as in her stocking feet she circled away from Freilicht and his mad eyes, shouting words she didn't hear, she was panicked yet calm with no time to recollect *You don't want to be hurt, —no you don't want to be hurt the way white people hurt black people* and she was backing away with the tongs upraised, as if that were a defense against the shotgun, as wavering and clumsy Freilicht leveled it at her, fully at her face, saying something incoherent-sounding like "—that's what you will, will you—you will, will you—yes?—eh?—whore—" as by design or accident he shifted the barrel so that when he pulled the triggers, and he pulled both triggers, the deafening blast was aimed at the window beside her and Calla this time was spared.

27

And then it was like we didn't belong to ourselves any more, like something had been started that couldn't be stopped.

Yes we kept a careful distance between us for I don't know how long but it didn't change things because everyone knew and that couldn't be erased and it got so I would hear him calling my name at night when he wasn't anywhere near, sometimes when I'd given up on him too and vowed I would forget but when I saw him again he told me the same thing with him, the same exact thing he said— "It's like it can't be stopped except by one way."

I never asked what that way would be.

28

Those months through the width of the Chautauqua Valley three hundred miles from east to west and up into the mountains and downstate as far as the Pennsylvania border people told of Calla and Tyrell Thompson without knowing their names: a wild red-haired white woman who had abandoned her children to run off with a black man, in some versions of the tale as it fructified like vegetation in steamy heat the white woman's husband and his kin were tracking them down meaning to kill them, in some versions of the tale the black man was an ex-convict from the South pretending to be a Christian minister carrying a Bible in one hand and a dowsing rod in the other—a dowsing rod that never failed to find water no matter how rocky or clayey the soil—and, strapped to one of his calves hidden up inside a trouser leg, an eight-inch deadly-sharp knife with which he'd slit the throats of many a white man between Georgia and here.

In fact, he'd slit the throat of the woman's husband.

In fact, the husband had tracked him down and killed him with a double-barreled shotgun.

In fact, the white woman had come home abandoned by her black lover and there she'd given birth to his baby, a coal-black creature, black and sinister as the Devil, and she'd gone crazy seeing it and the family had taken it away at once to do which of several things with it, no one knew for sure: give it to a Negro orphanage in Buffalo, or deliver it to the black man himself living in some slum tenement or dirt-floor shanty with his own wife and barefoot children or maybe did they out of shame and meanness drown the creature in the river?—yes but there endured a version of this tale that for all its being wholly illogical and even comic was nonetheless stubbornly told and retold for decades until it was finally unattached to any specific individuals or even to any specific locale except the Chautauqua backcountry in the old days when even normally law-abiding Christians were capable of such extravagances of behavior: *the outraged family had drowned the baby in their well . . . the very well the black man had helped them dig.*

There were stories and rumors less cruelly fantastical,

thus more vexing in their own way since they might be believed even by people who knew the Freilichts: such as, George's wife came from a white trash family up around Milburn with a history of alcoholism and mental instability, her own mother had run off after she was born leaving her to be brought up by her father and now it was being said that Calla had had a mental collapse and the family was trying to keep it a secret, wouldn't call in a doctor for her and wouldn't allow anyone to see her including her own relatives in Shaheen, unless it was Calla herself who wouldn't see them, wouldn't see anyone including her own children *And that's the insult of it, how always it comes back to a woman being a "good" mother in the world's eyes or a "bad" mother, how everything in a woman's life is funneled through her body between her legs.* Yet it was said, too, that Calla was still seeing Tyrell Thompson, going sometimes on foot to beg a ride with someone to Derby poor thing like she'd been bitten by a rabid creature so the craziness was in her blood for him, a rumor circulated that the family was going to commit her to the state hospital at Erie especially now she was drinking and they couldn't control her and Tyrell Thompson was a known drinker too, belligerent and dangerous, and still she was slipping away to see him, the two of them turning up in Derby, in Yewville, in Tintern Falls, in the lowest of lowlife taverns which were the only places people like that could be seen together *Because it's unnatural and disgusting, the races mixed like that just to look at it you feel sick.* And one of George Freilicht's cousins not otherwise known for his irresponsibility or excitability swore he'd seen Calla and Tyrell Thompson together on the Fourth of July, the two of them laughing together strolling by the river in Derby their arms around each other's waist behaving as if they'd been drinking and didn't give a damn for who saw them out in public displaying themselves like that *Like they were inviting trouble and were surely going to get it.*

In fact, as the Freilichts knew, Calla had been home with her family on that day, she'd been home with her family for weeks, impassive, silent, moving like a ghost among them. As if she had no physical being *like we didn't even belong to ourselves any longer, just parts scattered like animal carcasses the dogs have torn at* since Freilicht had aimed the shotgun at her and in a way she'd died but George Freilicht's cousin not otherwise known for his irresponsibility or excitability insisted he had seen her, yes he'd seen her, cavorting there in public with her black lover Tyrell Thompson.

29

Among the lurid tales of those months when the lovers were apart there was one that was true, and Calla perceived as true, because so terrible.

In the heat of a summer night in Derby, Tyrell Thompson was hunted down by a gang of drunken white men, beaten and kicked and stripped of his clothes, and his ankles bound with cord and they'd pushed him off a bridge into the Chautauqua River yelling, "See can you save yourself, water dowser," and "See how you like white women where you're going, nigger," and they stood at the railing watching as Tyrell Thompson began to drown, sinking, then surfacing, keeping himself afloat by the sheer desperate struggle of his arms, and he held his head erect like a seal refusing to drown, to die, to be bested, and as the current carried him downstream he managed to untie his ankles until at last before the eyes of astonished witnesses the man began swimming, saved himself from a drowning death *As if it was true, what he'd always boasted—water was his friend and in his power* just swimming away downstream and off into the night, and where he came staggering and panting to shore a mile or so down below the railroad yard and the slaughterhouses along the debris- and waste-befouled shore of the Negro section of town, no one of those white men on the bridge could see.

And hearing this story told her surreptitiously by a young woman cousin from Shaheen, Calla burst into bitter tears, the first tears of her adulthood, not simply because Tyrell Thompson had been so cruelly treated and so courageous but because, hearing of his cruel treatment and of his courage, Calla knew she had no choice but to see him again.

And what he wanted to do with her, what he would expect of her as his woman, she would have no choice, she would have no will, except to acquiesce.

30

They met by the river, they made love, fierce, wordless, wanting to hurt, Calla clutched Tyrell Thompson tight to her and in her smelling his sweet-sour whiskey breath and knowing long before she had reason to know that, yes now she was pregnant: now, at last, seed taken into her she wanted, now she was capable of such easy tears. *Why you cryin, honey, you just make the both of us feel bad.* And he'd gripped her throat in his huge hands not to choke her nor even to frighten her and not seemingly to silence her but—perhaps—to suggest the idea of silence to her so Calla would carry the imprint of his fingers on her skin, the weight of those fingers defining her very bones, for the remainder of her life. *Ain't nobody forcing you to love me, honey, don't you know that, smart white woman like you?*

That night when Calla became pregnant with Tyrell Thompson's child the western sky above the river was banked in clouds like gigantic boulders, or human brains, stacked thick, high, ponderous, massive, terrible to see. A mist lifted thinly from the water and invisible loons were calling to one another in harsh melancholy shreds of sound and all the way back to the house, to her home, stumbling, wiping hard at her eyes with her knuckles, Calla could see herself on her knees in the wet grass and there was Tyrell Thompson rising and swaying above her adjusting his clothing, she heard his lightly mocking murmurous words, the whiskey rhythm beneath them, she saw his fumbling fingers and felt again their hard sure hinting touch *But I love you, I would die for you, you only you you you* but it was a touch that released her finally and not without tenderness. How tall, how big his body, he was bareheaded and his tight kinky oily hair fitted his head snug as a cap defining its size, suggesting its weight, she saw the whites of his large intelligent eyes moving in their sockets smooth as grease. She wished he'd strangled her: that would be an ending. She could not bear it that since loving Tyrell Thompson she'd become one of those women she had always scorned, quick to tears, bones like water, raw and demeaning hunger shining in her face *Love me, love me don't ever stop I will die if you stop* and maybe in fact Tyrell Thompson did have a wife, a black woman with whom she lived in Derby when the mood struck him, maybe he had a number of women, and more children than he could recall, in the river towns he visited on foot making his restless way from east to west and from west to east dowsing for water or plying whatever trade might nourish him from one season to the next, as he'd hinted— cardplaying, gambling, blacksmithing, livery stable hand, common laborer *like my daddy before me and his daddy before him God's progeny can't all be lilies of the field white and pure and blessed Oh no ma'am we can't.*

31

In continual quarrel with him Calla murmured aloud, "—I didn't choose the color of my skin, how can I be *blamed*." And, "No more than you I can't be blamed." Yet unspoken between them was the understanding that she would come to him, when he wanted her.

Now she was pregnant the heedlessness of a true pregnancy was upon her. Not the sick dull vague resigned and merely physical pregnancies of her early marriage but a fevered condition by day and by night as if she held a giant seashell pressed against her ear, its roaring always with her, thus she was incautious in remarks she sometimes made aloud that might be overheard by others, knowledge of her secret self carried away from her and out of her power, to be used against her. It was not even that her condition was a secret so much as the fact that to Calla it had nothing to do with anyone apart from Tyrell Thompson and herself, how then could she speak of it, or wish to speak of it, to others.

She thought obsessively of the man who was her lover, her lover now mysteriously inside her, carried safe inside her, protected by the warmth of her very flesh, yet she rarely allowed herself to think of Tyrell Thompson as a man among men, a black man among white men in a world as steeped in racial injustice as in the unacknowledged breathable element of air, a world she might ignore as it touched upon herself—her, Calla, "George Freilicht's wife"—yet could hardly ignore as it touched upon Tyrell

Thompson. For in that world all the man might be outwardly was defined for him and granted him by his enemies, as the finest bred racehorse no matter its beauty, its
strength, its courage, its speed, is defined and limited by
the space of the intolerable penned corral or pasture into
which his owners have forced him.

"—why didn't you strangle me then, that would have
been an ending."

But she didn't mean it of course.

For never had Calla Honeystone been happier.

Outwardly during this fevered interim of about eight
weeks in the fall of 1912 Calla behaved tractably, cooper-
atively, with no sign of resistance or sullenness or even of
recalling, in Freilicht's embarrassed presence, the fact that
he had threatened her life. Husband and wife were cour-
teous to each other, like convalescents. Elderly but ever-
vigilant and ever-suspicious Mrs. Freilicht wondered if
Calla was repentant of her sins and hopeful of making
amends—a woman of surpassing vanity, she would allow
herself to be courted by her husband's wife.

Calla was suffused with the bloom of pregnancy: she
was well: did not listen to much of what the Freilichts told
her or discussed in her presence but still she heard, un-
failingly she heard, and threw herself with energy and even
zest into those mindless mechanical household chores that
allowed her a fierce and undivided concentration upon her
interior life. The most seemingly communal tasks Calla
made into solitary occupations; there was something almost voluptuous in her absorption in the dumbly tactile,

the close-at-hand. Only the intrusion of others—of her children, her Freilicht children as she thought them—threw her into disequilibrium. Looking up from the limp bloodless pimpled carcass of, say, a butchered chicken she was cleaning on the back porch, her mind miles away, Calla would see her little girl Emmaline, who'd just spoken to her, or asked a question of her she had no idea how to answer since she hadn't heard and had no wish to hear. A smile, a quick kiss, a pretty frowning admonition—"Momma is busy, dear, why don't you run along and play with—" her mind already releasing the child to that sublunary vagueness, that dim uncharted periphery of household inhabitants or guests or visitors or pets Calla had rarely, since coming there to live, made the slightest effort to know.

32

Emmaline a half-century later: "Did I hate her?—no, she was my mother. I only lived in terror that she would finally go away."

33

And then so abruptly, when her lover summoned her, she did go away.

Though saying beforehand to Freilicht, "—Let me go: I won't take anything," but Freilicht stiffened in rage, hurt, resignation, saying, "You'll take everything," so softly Calla could barely make out his words. His eyes shone a sickish yellow, his weatherworn face was creased as if it had been crumpled, cruelly, by hand; Calla thought, staring at him, *Does he love me after all? But why?*

She was in a hurry. She was too distracted for pity.

Impatiently she cried, "—I'm pregnant with another man's child."

And turned her back on him, and walked away. And if Freilicht wished at that moment that he had in fact killed her with his shotgun, yes and turned the gun then on himself, Calla could not know, had no time to consider, Calla was already gone.

34

They met behind the ruins of the old cider mill, they made love there, a final time, had no intention of falling upon each other as they did with such desperation, such need—but that was what happened. And afterward sitting so close together in the shade of the collapsed building amid the drunken hum of bees and wasps and flies above the sweet-reeking landslide of apple compost it was as if they drank from the same bottle, the same unmarked whiskey bottle, with the same mouth.

Calla had not known what her lover meant, at first. Something about a rowboat he'd found upstream. Or had he maybe stolen it?—"Ain't nobody going to miss the old scrubby thing till it's too late."

Calla had not known if she was being tested as to her courage. As to whether, set beside a Negro woman, the women of the kind Tyrell Thompson knew, she would be found lacking, no true match for a man of Tyrell Thompson's quality, she was reckless in any case, excited with love and lovemaking and her lover so close beside her after weeks of deprivation when she'd half feared she would never see him again so she said, love-warmed and whiskey-warmed nudging her head against his hard enough to give them each a little bolt of pain, "—You think I won't do it?" liking perhaps the impromptu nature of it, the defiance, the flaunting and self-display and madness of it, the two of them rowing downstream to Tintern Falls on a day when anyone might see them who chose to see them, setting their course deliberately for the falls at Tintern that had not the power—so he boasted, or gave the air of boasting—to withstand Tyrell Thompson's God-given mastery over water.

Or maybe he just wanted to kill them both. And this, so extravagant a way of making an ending.

Calla said, "You think I won't do it, damn you?—is that what you think?"

Tyrell Thompson said, laughing, "Sure you will, honey."

Calla said, "I will. I'll do it."

Tyrell Thompson said, "Sure you will, honey. Just like that."

Calla said, her voice rising, "God damn you I *will*."

She'd told him, earlier, lying in his arms in the shade of a collapsed wall of the mill, about the baby-to-be. And she'd felt him—was it stiffen? shiver? stifle a spasm of laughing?—and take it all in silence, not a word.

Calla cried, "Oh you bastard you'll see!" scrambling to her feet leaning heavily against Tyrell Thompson who grabbed at her hips laughing and they wrestled together fondly and a little roughly and then they were making love again, harder and with less ceremony than before, and Calla screamed and clutched at her lover so close against her she could not see his face, her eyes shut tight against his face as the huge man pumped his life's blood into her, groaning and burrowing helpless as a resentful child, "Uh-uh-*uh*," he moaned forcing her by painful little inches backward in the dirt until at last it was over and Calla lay dazed, tears running from the corners of her pinched eyes and her entire body aching as if she'd been flung from a great height to lie here spread-eagled and powerless on her back trusting to a giant of a black man not to smash her bones to bits or smother her with his weight and though now he was saying how he loved her *Oh honey oh honey* she felt her consciousness close to extinction seeing overhead the sky lightly fleeced with clouds, layer upon layer of pale clouds, so empty, so without consolation or even the illusion of such, Calla felt her mouth shaping an involuntary smile.

When had I stopped believing in, what is it — God? — and Jesus Christ His only begotten son? After loving Tyrell Thompson, or before?

She made her way through the prickly underbrush to where he'd dragged the rowboat up onto the red-clayey bank of the creek, the creek was only two or three feet deep at this point so he'd simply waded in it: and there the rowboat was: larger than Calla had expected, maybe twelve feet in length, unpainted, moderately weathered and splintery to the touch and there was a puddle of brackish water in it but the oars were in good condition and the seats had been strengthened recently, fresh boards nailed across, certainly this was a boat that belonged to someone, a fisherman's boat, some farmer or his son who lived close by, so Tyrell Thompson had stolen it, certainly. Calla drew her hand tentatively across the hull, Calla swallowed hard. The beat beat beat of the pulse in her loins seemed to her so powerful and so terrible she could not endure it. She squinted at where Tyrell Thompson in his somber black attire was crouched incongruously in the stream, trouser legs rolled up, stooping to wash his face in his cupped hands, she called out harshly, gaily, " —I told you: I'm ready."

And so they set out.

And so, once their course was set, they would not turn back.

The creek, a nameless creek, would empty into the

Chautauqua River five or six miles to the north and once on the Chautauqua at a point about parallel with Milburn they would make their way swiftly and unerringly past Flemingville, past Shaheen, toward Tintern Falls and wherever it was they were going. The single bottle of whiskey which would have to do for them for hours in the pitiless September sun was still three-quarters full, which was a good thing.

If this is a dream it is not my dream for how should I know the language in which to dream it.

35

So, there, on the river, in the slanted sunshine, the stolen weatherworn rowboat bucking the waves with a look almost of gaiety, defiance. Yes certainly defiance: the big broad-shouldered black man at the oars rowing not quite rhythmically but with strength, purpose, deliberation, the oars lifting dripping from the water and sinking again at once; with a look both antic and violent, and facing him her knees nudging his knees, the white woman with the long tattered wind-whipped red hair, a blaze of it in the sun as she sat so unnaturally straight in a posture of amazement or delight or terror or simple childlike entrancement staring at the wide river so much wider, and rougher, than you know from shore, and watching the tangled banks that seemed to be passing in drunken spasms, and now they were beyond the mill at Flemingville the very sawmill at which Mr. Honeystone had worked when his farm failed him and shortly thereafter came the houses at Shaheen so oddly, illicitly glimpsed from their rears, lightning rods, glass winking in windows, clothes and white-glaring linens hanging from clotheslines, and there was the high-arched Shaheen bridge with its nightmare spidery look, floorboards that rattled when wagons were drawn across it, rivets glinting coldly in the sun and everything perceived as unfamiliar from Calla's new lowered angle of vision on the river and what was Tyrell Thompson saying to her?—telling her another time as if he'd forgotten he'd told her before about his young mother years before he was born, fourteen years old she'd been taken by night by slavery abolitionists across the Potomac at Martinsburg, Virginia, taken from house to house with a small group of terrified young slaves and finally into the large farmhouse of a Quaker family in Pennsylvania and from there to New York State and onto a railroad running up through the northern part of the state to the Canadian border thus out of the reach of slave catchers, and the white railroad workers were ready to help—for a fee, and so Tyrell Thompson came north sixteen years before he was born, and who his momma's people were back down in Virginia he was never to know, never even to inquire, and Calla returned his hard grimace of a smile, their knees companionably nudging, sweat in rivulets running down their faces like tears as, now, they were beginning at last to attract serious attention on shore, men in shirtsleeves by the dock behind a granary staring at them shading their eyes to see who they were, this defiant

mismatched couple *A nigger and a white woman! — look!* and
Tyrell Thompson did not slacken in his vigorous rowing,
his tight-fitting black coat straining across his muscular
shoulders as he rowed taking pleasure in the ache of his
body in the mindlessness of such effort, and Calla saw
this, Calla drank from the whiskey bottle and passed it
back to Tyrell Thompson with his fine-scarred purplish-
red black skin, a skin that looked many-layered and not
thin like Calla's, she smiled refusing to beg her lover to
change his mind and very likely in her mesmerized state
she did not want him to change his mind, she was in dread
of him turning coward in her place *I do what I do, what I
have done is what I have wanted to do* she saw he was perspiring big oily globules of sweat, his coat and shirt soaked in
sweat, and what a fine rancid odor lifted from him, the
cuffs of his trousers wet as well, like the soiled hem of
Calla's skirt, they smiled and winked at each other, Calla
bumped his knees hard with her own and leaned forward
precipitously to seize his face between her hands and kiss
the lips greedily and the snubbed oily nose, she made a
gesture of licking his sweat-begrimed forehead but the
boat was lurching and Tyrell Thompson urged her gently
back onto the seat *I wanted to scream and scream, scream my
legs wrapped around him to squeeze the very life from him* and
Calla relented seeing how her skin was visibly burning
from the sun, she stared seeing the luminous pale-freckled
skin turning pink in the humid sunshine and she thought
with regret of how her face would peel, shredded and
scarified like the beginning of death when her enemies laid
her out gloating to contemplate her one final time praying
God to have mercy on her sluttish unredeemed soul.

Not far east of Tintern Falls there came hurtled at
the couple in the bucking rowboat isolated shouts, crude
warnings but they were aloof to the commands of strangers; the woman meant to maintain till the very end her stiff
alert posture; the black man hunched, rowing, and then
straight, his shoulders straightening in pride meaning to
resist the natural tug of his bones toward the earth, then
again hunched with the effort of maneuvering the boat
always a little faster than it could go, and now in the
suddenly frothy rapids above the falls the little boat began
seriously to dip, to plunge, to shudder, to cavort, so that
Tyrell Thompson's smile looked startled for a perceptible
instant and Calla felt that stabbing vertigo in the pit of the
belly that signals acute danger but she gripped both sides
of the boat and steadied herself as with drunken swiftness
they flew beneath the bridge at Tintern Falls where faces
gaped down at them, white faces, men, a boy or two, arms
and fists were waved, the air rang with shouts of warning
and upset and incredulity, but the couple in the boat paid
no heed, it was queenly and kingly, their defiance of all
who witnessed their flight and were bound to speak of the
spectacle for years, decades, lifetimes, still they paid no
heed to strangers, looking at each other their eyes drowning in each other as the roar of the falls ahead began by odd
fast jumps to increase in volume more rapidly than one
might expect and the sky had dissolved in white spray and
froth and the world was finite enough now to fit inside a
twelve-foot battered rowboat stolen out of a marshy inlet
and Calla thought *I'm ready* and Tyrell Thompson by now
had carefully lifted the oars to place them in the oarlocks
so he might be observed should witnesses care to observe

him sitting erect and alert and unafraid his arms folded across his broad chest and his big hands tight beneath his armpits, not a glimmer of apprehension in that stoic masklike face, not a glimmer of apprehension in the woman's face so if you were a witness to this spectacle at Tintern Falls in September 1912 you knew and could hardly not know how these two were a couple bonded in love, and more than love.

PART
III

It is the remainder of her life of which I find it so difficult to speak: except to see her shut her door, lock her door upon herself, one of those large drafty rooms at the top of the old farmhouse, but not a room she was obliged to share with her husband or with anyone and which only at rare intervals during the subsequent years were visitors, even her children, allowed to enter.

My mother has said *People lived differently then, they did things for life, made gestures that lasted for life* and it was fifty-five years Calla chose to remain in seclusion in that farmhouse that was never home to her, caring to leave the house and the property no more than a half-dozen times and each of these times exclusively for the purpose of attending a funeral, the final occasion being March 1928 when her husband died and was buried in the hilly cemetery behind the First Lutheran Church of Shaheen beneath a granite marker already engraved to include *Beloved Wife Edith* 1890— .

She would die finally in 1967 at the age of seventy-seven by which time she had outlived her husband by thirty-nine years and her lover by fifty-five years and I think how quaint, how diminished they must have seemed to her by then, like images seen through the wrong end of a telescope but perhaps I am mistaken for how can I speak of that woman let alone speak for her who scarcely knew her: she who was my mother's mother yet as distant to me as any stranger.

Because I was mad, or because I was never mad?

I cannot bear to think of her yet I think of her continuously.

I cannot solve the puzzle, the riddle, the mystery she

embodies: Calla Honeystone, a young woman at the time of her initial retreat, from all that I've been able to learn only semi-invalided and intermittently unwell (both her legs were broken in the plunge over the falls, one kneecap seriously shattered, and there were many lacerations, and, to come, migraine headaches and spells of blindness and "fits") yet she chose to withdraw inside the Freilicht household and inside the farmhouse itself—roof, walls, windows—to define herself as, not Edith Freilicht, for she was never apparently that woman, but a presence of no distinctive name or being or volition or wish, performing household chores with an unfailing concentration and indifference, coming downstairs from time to time—when not "unwell"—to sit at the table with the others, even to make a polite pretense of showing interest in grandchildren as they were presented to her, though without troubling to remember names, for what after all are names, to what purpose the distinction of individuals, what futility, vanity *It isn't that one day resembles the preceding day, or the following day, in your room at the top of the house dreaming at your high window watching the river through the trees glittering like a snake's scales but one day is in fact that day, all days are identical.*

Once when I was a small child three or four years old my mother had driven back to that place she called home, her mouth downward turning around the word *home,* the very sound of it, like *family* too, like *mother,* the old farmhouse of dim red weatherworn but still sturdy brick at the end of a snow-bordered lane of pines so straight and so tall they seemed to reach into the sky beyond my range of vision craning my neck in the car, and it was the week following Christmas and I'd climbed the stairs to see what it was I'd been warned against disturbing and there was my mother's mother's door ajar at the end of the hall, perhaps two inches ajar, as if in invitation, the woman shy, shy inside the chill averted gaze and the face both ravaged and beautiful, the bones sharp in the cheeks and socketing the eyes and the hair metallic gray carelessly braided and left to hang between the gaunt shoulder blades like a noose and I crept to the door and looked inside smelling a faint odor of camphor and there in the twilit textured light my grand-mother's pale face, her figure, dark-clad, shading into the shadows of the room or into the very wallpaper, but there seemed for an instant to pass between us a small stab of recognition *Because we are linked by blood and blood is memory without language* and she spoke to me questioningly, her voice harsh as if it had been unused for some time, very likely she was asking if I would like to come into her room but I shrank away my fingers jammed in my mouth and ran downstairs and beyond that the memory dissolves in a mist of childish shame and adult regret *Because we are linked by blood, thus irrevocably.*

Never did she speak to the Freilichts of Tyrell Thompson, nor did they speak to her of him. Of the baby—the baby-to-be—the bloody miscarriage amid the catastrophe of the plunge over the falls, the smashed row-boat, the flailing drowning broken bodies, of course no one spoke and *no one was ever to speak.*

In families there are frequently matters of which no one speaks, nor even alludes. There are no words for these matters. As the binding skeleton beneath the flesh is never acknowledged by us and, when at last it defines itself, is after all an obscenity.

How have I come by this knowledge: by way of fragments, whispers, half-heard reproaches. In point of fact as I was growing up I heard of my mother's mother the "crazy" woman as much from girlfriends and from their mothers as I did from my own mother, for to her, Emmaline, the mystery of Calla Honeystone was a deep and abiding embarrassment. Years before Calla died in 1967 Emmaline would say *Let the dead past bury the dead* it was a fervent prayer for her, an appeal to God and His sense of fair play.

She shut her door, she locked her door upon herself early in the winter of 1913 as soon as she'd sufficiently recovered from the trauma done to her body, able to walk with difficulty yet with stubborn persistence using a cane and her thin shoulders hunched, head bowed to protect her watery squinty eyes from the sun glaring fierce as a razor on the dullest of surfaces, and ever after that as the seasons reeled past, the years, the decades, Canada geese flying north above the highest peak of the highest roof of the house, Canada geese flying south issuing their hoarse melancholy cries, and the invisible loons on the river, and the warning calls of red-winged blackbirds in the marshes, moons too flying by, twin moons reflected calmly in her wide calm staring eyes as she thought *No hunger is ever satisfied if it is a true hunger.*

She believed that river water remained in her lungs, the dark brackish taste of it, the faint scent of vomit.

She'd vomited convulsively when they dragged her to shore. Her broken useless legs, her hair trailing like seaweed in the churning white water, eyeballs rolled up in her head like a great doll's so she hadn't been a witness to what was whispered later through the valley, that the men had allowed Tyrell Thompson to drown there amid the boulders and the screaming white rapids *No but he slipped through our fingers, big black bastard got away his head split like a pumpkin spilling brains* but they'd relented, finally dragging him from the water a half-mile downstream, his broken battered body like the carcass of an animal floating in the river for days, the stink and heaviness of death lifting from it and where the water dowser was buried, and who mourned him, which black woman, or women, how many children scattered in the river towns east to west and west to east along the Chautauqua no whites were to know, certainly not the white woman who had nearly died with him at Tintern, plunging over the falls with him in a rowboat that had shattered about them like kindling tossed up shrieking amid the granite rocks and boulders and the cascading white water rabid with froth like old men's beards as she'd think of it afterward mute and broken her bones in traction in a city hospital where for some time she was not expected to recover until one whitely glaring morning her eyelids fluttered open and Calla woke to full horrific consciousness and began screaming *Just screaming and screaming what you wouldn't ever expect from the lips of a woman like that: "Jesus! Jesus! Jesus!"*

Fifty-five years.

A life split in two but not in half, the weight of it in the past and all that remained a protracted repetition of minutes, of peace. As standing at a high window as night comes on you observe how by slow ineluctable degrees the outer world diminishes and your own reflection defines itself without color, or texture, or depth, or soul. *Did you know it was Death that summoned you, a dowsing rod in his hand? Or was it Love? And were you faithful to him however bitterly however purposelessly all the days of your long life? Or did you forget him, and this inevitably, helplessly, as, as life passes through the seasons, the decades, the calm mad minutes of the ticking of household clocks, we are bound to forget, all, everything, our very selves?*

Still she stands there, at the high window with its view of the river a quarter-mile away, as night comes on.

Once my mother divorced the man who was, who is, my father, and left him behind in Shaheen, and moved away to a city at the western border of the state, the visits back home were infrequent and were primarily visits with my mother's brother Edward and his family, my thick-set kindly taciturn uncle Edward who had inherited the farm when his father died of a massive coronary in 1928 and who did quite well with it relative to his farming neighbors once he shrewdly sold off half the acreage and kept the most fertile and tillable land for himself in addition to

long lovely sloping stretches of deciduous woods and pas-
tureland along the Chautauqua River: Edward Freilicht
grew wheat, soybeans, and corn, razed the old rotting
orchards and laid in acres of Cortland apples and Bing
cherries, rebuilt the old barns, refenced the pastures, reno-
vated part of the old farmhouse and painted its tall narrow
shutters an unexpected white, and became at about the
time of his mother's death in 1967 an officer of the New
York State Farm Bureau to whom state legislators were
obliged to listen with a modicum of respect. My mother
and Edward were not much alike (my mother often said
she'd resembled, she'd been adoring of, their older brother,
Enoch, who had been killed in the Philippines in World
War II) nor did they give any outward appearance of being
sentimental people but they were linked of course by
family obligations, family history, family memory and
expiations, they were avid to speak together *And how is
Mother? Unchanged? Always unchanged? — it's the others of us
who change isn't it?* in privacy together while sometimes
through an entire visit of two or three days my mother's
mother would remain out of sight, there might be creak-
ing floorboards overhead and we'd imagine a sound, a
hesitant contemplative sound, of footsteps on the stairs
descending and then abruptly retreating back up to whatever it was there in her room under the eaves furnished so
sparely yet so seemingly completely, where when I was a
girl of fourteen and fifteen I dreamt of her as a figure
static as the wallpaper of that room of which I'd had a
glimpse (I believed I'd had a glimpse: had memorized:
a lacy floral pattern of no discernible color overlaid upon a
pale background of no discernible color, the pattern in

vertical rows) since wallpaper consists of aesthetic config-
urations that appear to move even as they repeat themselves endlessly, a calm steady confining repetition from
wall to wall to wall to wall thus the prison of that room,
the sanctuary of that room, for a woman, for that woman,
perhaps for me since I am a woman, perhaps it is the
woman's womb, she is imprisoned there in her womb or is
it a sanctuary?—so I would offend my mother and my
uncle asking why my grandmother kept so much to herself, rarely stepped out of the house except to go into the
barns sometimes or the chicken coop, she hadn't left the
property itself in years and why, why if she wasn't actually
ill, wasn't mad, or senile, why didn't she at least visit
neighbors, relatives, go to church with the family?—and
they would assure me that my grandmother had been
offered many opportunities to leave the house, to visit
anywhere she wished, there was a tacit understanding that
her son would drive her anywhere but no one wanted to
anger her by making these suggestions that had been made
countless times over the years and the fact was that the
woman lived the life she chose, she was happy in that life
and it was no one's business after all but her own, my
uncle's face darkening with blood as he spoke, my mother's
fair fine skin pink as if smarting yet still I persisted, for I
thought it such a horror, such a grief, yes and an embarrassment too, I said, "She's made a prison of this house, it's
like she's a nun, it must be to punish herself," and my
mother said quietly, angrily, "You don't know—what do
you know! People do what they want to do."

But I could not, could not believe that terrible truth,
don't expect me to believe such a terrible truth, it's pitiless,

it leaves no room for mercy, it isn't the world as I would have imagined it.

In the Chautauqua area it was generally believed that Calla had gone mad: not raving mad but quietly, even placidly mad, as women sometimes did, women of her generation, or the generations preceding, worn out with childbirth or female maladies whose very Latin names evoked distaste, of course there were madmen too, living alone on isolated farms in the foothills or at the outskirts of one or another slowly developing town, recluses, hermits, the men living alone in ramshackle farmhouses or log cabins or tarpaper shanties or in some desperate instances in old packing cases in the township dump, while the women tended to withdraw within actual households often with the implicit support or encouragement of husbands, parents, children, ministers, parish priests willing to come to the house to deliver communion and to pray with the afflicted party, who might in truth not be considered afflicted but perversely independent, blessed, requiring nothing of the profane world's vanity but subsisting within the walls of a single house a single household performing the routine and wholly satisfying mindless tasks of housewifery, as Calla did once she was recovered from the worst of her trauma, her old zeal returning, her former rapt concentration, those strong deft fingers, rather muscular arms, a predilection for such solitary tasks as ironing clothes, scrubbing floors, polishing furniture and silverware and washing windows and sewing, at first by hand and then at the wonderful little gleaming black

Singer sewing machine with the foot pedal and the flying needle with its eye so curiously at its point: just to watch that needle was bliss! *Like the flash of heat lightning that tells you all that is, is now.*

Yet it was not true that Calla kept solely to herself, within even a year of the scandalous incident at Tintern Falls. Often she was to be found working companionably with her female in-laws, especially at the preparation of meals (and especially at harvest when Freilicht would have hired on as many as twelve extra hands), and it so strangely developed that the elderly Mrs. Freilicht who had endured years of perpetual disapproval and outrage regarding her headstrong daughter-in-law became not only forgiving of the young woman but protective of her now she was broken and humbled and even her beauty marred by rivulets of tears, or were they scars, or stains, if it was not a genuine Christian repentance that glimmered in those eyes it had the look of one *Praise be to God from Whom all blessings flow, praise Father, Son, and Holy Ghost that a sinner is returned to the fold!* thus among the reversals of Calla's life came this odd belated flowering, though almost entirely unvoiced, of a deep maternal interest on the part of the elder woman whose strength of will and indefatigable energy allowed her dominance in her son's household well into her eighty-sixth year and whose brief illness and collapse and death Calla was to mourn with the shock of fresh grief as if she had thought, still so young, hardly thirty years old, that one death, one violent bitter loss, was all that God would have required of her forever.

When Calla accompanied the family to church, and to Mrs. Freilicht's gravesite, dressed entirely in black, a black veil covering her face from forehead to chin, leaning on George Freilicht's arm, moving stiffly, her gaze downcast and unreadable, it was the first time church members and neighbors had seen her for years: since the incident at Tintern Falls and Calla's return to the Freilichts and what was generally if vaguely understood to be her "strangeness": and it would be years, in fact eight years, before they had the satisfaction of seeing her again, this time at Freilicht's funeral and burial, at which occasion she, just widowed, seeming scarcely to have changed since Mrs. Freilicht's death, would be dressed again entirely in black, a shapeless oversized black linen coat borrowed from a sister-in-law, a black straw hat and a coarse black veil covering her face from forehead to chin, Calla this time leaning on her elder son Enoch's arm and yielding to curious eyes no outward sign of grief or of the stoic suppression of grief so they, those others whose faces, let alone names, she had never troubled to learn, murmured together in communal outrage and gratification *Look at her! so young! she'll outlive them all! she'll inherit! all that land! she'll take up with another nigger and bring him home and this time she'll have nigger babies right here in Shaheen with nobody to stop her!* which turned out to be utterly utterly mistaken.

After her death (quietly in her sleep of heart failure, one May night in 1967, no warning beforehand: she appeared a young seventy-seven) the family discovered her girlhood Bible left open on her bureau, the tissue-thin pages dog-eared and worn with a look of having been read repeatedly so it was a consolation to the Freilichts to think that she had had faith, still, in God, in the Christian religion, and particularly in the teachings of Martin Luther, in the forgiveness of sins and the redemption of sinners through Jesus Christ our Savior, for all the Freilichts and their kin and farming neighbors were un-questioning Christians in those days *I asked him do you believe in God? —just tell me and he shrugged his shoulders wide as the length of another man's arm and laughed and said, Why certainly, honey, you know I believe in God: had better, so I said, You're lying, you're too smart to believe in any god white men have got up in their own image, so he made this snorting laughing noise of his like a horse almost, I knew I had him now, I had him now, so he granted I was right, he said, Now look: a white man's god ain't much certainly but he's a whole lot better than nothing, to keep them white men from the full nastiness they'd naturally like to be* which was their way of redressing certain imbalances in life, for instance sinners who suffered insufficiently in this world would suffer sufficiently, and forever, in that other world, and the uncomplaining faithful, meek and mild and abrogating their militancy to formal govern-ments, armies, legislated laws, would inherit what re-mained, and even if in so many —so many!—instances the balm of Eternity might not erase the heartbreak of Time these good Lutherans would at least know that their Savior knew, they would at least know that their Savior knew.

For long spells of the life that remained stretching out seemingly without end Calla was physically disoriented; inhabiting her body as if it were another's; in such stasis pain came at unpredictable intervals sharp and stabbing as a bird's beak and she would lie motionless as a dead woman on her bed in that room sequestered beneath the eaves, a damp cloth over her eyes to assuage the curious pain that rose and broke, rose and broke, rose and broke like cascades of glittering white water in which she yearned to drown except her strong lungs refused to fill, choking and vomiting she rid herself of it repeatedly yet lay unmoving on the horsehair mattress beneath the wool-and-silk quilt of three hundred sixty-five squares her mother-in-law had sewed for her in her first illness when it was clear that Calla Honeystone was broken and could not ever mend properly, thus she lay floating as beyond her locked door the clocks of the household ticked their smug time and her children grew older not by degrees it seemed but in sudden pleats and jumps, their faces hard with bone as her own, their eyes wary, intelligent, evasive, Enoch and Edward and Emmaline were their names but these were not sacred names Calla whispered to herself in moods of distress as a mother might, nor did she whisper the name of her late husband George Freilicht except to regret at the time of his death that she had not been able to love him as any man of his strength and industry and Christian charity deserved, and there was too the elderly woman whom she had never called Mother, now dead, and beyond the locked door of her room the century rushed headlong as over a series of cataracts into its future of wars, financial collapse, boom times, and new presidents of the United States, and new wars, and the area around Shaheen acquiring roads paved in asphalt, the River Road itself at the end of the Freilicht's quarter-mile lane not only paved but widened considerably, and there were motorcars and no longer horse-drawn wagons, there were tractors and no longer horse-drawn plows, there were combines, and threshers, and telephones, and radios, and television, newspaper headlines and photographs flaring up as if, thrown onto the fire, they existed forever in that moment before con-sumption when every detail is irradiated as if from within and given the deluded significance of immortality, so Calla lived however disoriented and bemused and cynical at times and at other times simply grateful thinking *I was never unhappy, I regret nothing* for otherwise she would never have known him: her lover: whose name she did not say either as if doubting it had been the man's true name but she could see him distinctly outside the window, a stranger, down there holding his dowsing rod in both hands like a prayer at mid-chest, that trespasser, black suit fitting him tight in the shoulders and a frayed white shirt some woman had ironed and starched for him but not for a while, and that black bowler hat snug on his head and that light in his eyes like the ivory of old piano keys when she'd told him *My name is Calla.*

Yet for years they were seen together and tales of such sightings repeated, seen always at a distance so that their exact identities were in doubt yet everyone in the Chautau-qua Valley knew who the red-haired white woman and the giant of a black man were glimpsed at dusk walking together by the river their arms defiantly around each other's waist their smiling faces lowered together conspir-ing and then again in the ruins of the old mill above Shaheen where other illicit lovers sometimes met, or was it in Derby at the lower end of town in one or another riverside tavern or café where a black man with a white woman would not arouse immediate outrage or at least the violence that such outrage as cultivated by white men usually entailed, and yes of course on the Chautauqua itself they were frequently sighted in the doomed little rowboat, Tyrell Thompson rowing with that air of precision and desperation and the white woman gripping the sides of the boat in belated alarm for years, for decades until finally the descendants of the descendants of those individuals who had actually seen Calla and Tyrell Thompson on that day or who had at least heard firsthand breathless accounts from those who had were all dead, or had grown too infirm to remember, or had moved away from that remote region in upstate New York to which they might return if they chose to return only as temporary visitors: strangers.

That final time. The summer before her death and my mother and I were visiting the farm and so little seemed to have changed, I was sitting restless on the top step of the veranda a few feet away from her in the dusk, she was sitting in one of the high-backed wicker rockers but she wasn't rocking just sitting there still with one of the barn cats drowsy in her lap so I could hear the cat's low throaty purring and we didn't speak and my heart began to beat rapidly urging me to speak since I wasn't a child any longer, I was a young woman needing to ask of my mother's mother certain crucial questions before it was too late *for as each dies, a part of that old world dies with her* but I was wary of offending her, provoking her into rising and walking away stiff with arthritic dignity as I'd witnessed upon occasions when others however well-intentioned tried to draw Calla into casual conversation, I sat silent thinking *Was it for love you threw your life away?—did you throw your life away?* but I said nothing as darkness began to lift from the grass and the fireflies began winking in the shadows and suddenly there were dozens of them, hundreds, tiny lights beating and pulsing and the urge to confront my mother's mother subsided and after some minutes she remarked as if we'd been talking this way, the two of us, companionably, easily, all along, ". . . when I was a little girl, I went to school up in Milburn . . . a one-room school . . . in winter it got dark early so the teacher, Mrs. Vogel, lit our lanterns for us one by one so we could see our way home . . . and we'd be walking, a string of us, along the road . . . and the children would turn up onto lanes, or other roads, going over hills . . . the fireflies always remind me of that, the lanterns we'd carried . . . the lanterns going off across the hills and into the dark and I'd go on by myself, finally I was the last one on our road and by the time I got home it was night, and cold," and I sat there listening entranced for never had I heard my mother's mother speak in so prolonged and so purposeful a way, never to me, sitting there in the high-backed wicker rocker one of the Freilichts had built by hand a scruffy barn cat drowsing on her lap, though in the dim light I couldn't see her face just the outline of her glimmering hair, I said, "Grandmother, oh when was that?" and she replied after a pause as if she were bemused at my tone or maybe she was actually calculating, counting the years and it was that that bemused her, "—A long time ago."